Then Again, Maybe I Won't

Judy Blume spent her childhood in Elizabeth, New Jersey, making up stories inside her head. She has spent her adult years in many places, doing the same thing, only now she writes her stories down on paper. More than 82 million copies of her books have been sold, in thirty-two languages. Her twenty-eight books have won many awards, including the National Book Foundation's Medal for Distinguished Contribution to American Literature.

Judy lives in Key West, Florida, and New York City with her husband. She loves her readers and is happy to hear from them. You can visit her at JudyBlume.com, follow @JudyBlume on Twitter or join her at Judy Blume on Facebook.

Books by Judy Blume

Blubber
Iggie's House
Starring Sally J. Freedman as Herself
Are You There, God? It's Me, Margaret
It's Not the End of the World
Then Again, Maybe I Won't
Deenie
Just as Long as We're Together
Here's to You, Rachel Robinson

For older readers

Forever
Tiger Eyes
Letters to Judy: What Kids Wish They Could Tell You

For younger readers

The One in the Middle Is the Green Kangaroo
Freckle Juice

The Fudge books

Tales of a Fourth Grade Nothing
Otherwise Known as Sheila the Great
Superfudge
Fudge-a-Mania
Double Fudge

The Pain and the Great One series

On Wheels!
Go Places!

Then Again,
Maybe I Won't

JUDY
BLUME

MACMILLAN CHILDREN'S BOOKS
in association with Heinemann

First published in the US 1971 by Bradbury Press Inc.
First published in the UK 1979 by Pan Books Ltd

This edition published 2016 by Macmillan Children's Books
an imprint of Pan Macmillan
The Smithson, 6 Briset Street, London EC1M 5NR
EU representative: Macmillan Publishers Ireland Limited,
Mallard Lodge, Lansdowne Village, Dublin 4
Associated companies throughout the world
www.panmacmillan.com

ISBN 978-1-5098-0625-6

7 9 8

A CIP catalogue record for this book is available from
the British Library.

Printed and bound by CPI Group (UK) Ltd, Croydon CR0 4YY

For Dick

you'll have to tell the how I melted down to
nothing right on your front porch.
I walked away from her. Mrs Gorsky. She was
still banging on her window. Well, let her. I didn't
what so? What?
A long as it doesn't land in the
der year when I go to junior high. I do
my favourite sport. I just wish I w
long. It's important to be tall when you
basketball. You're that much
play on the Y all day Saturday an
Frankie Bollino, Joe Schartz
Turner. We call the two Joes 'Big
Poselli's
Maybe my boss will let me

Chapter 1

Who says March is supposed to come in like a lion and go out like a lamb? That's a lot of bull. All it's done this March is rain. I'm sick of it.

'Hey Tony . . .' Mrs Gorsky yelled from her upstairs window.

I pretended not to hear her. I took a *Jersey Journal* out of my sack and tossed it onto her front porch. *Pow-Pow-Pow* I got you Mrs Gorsky! Now you can't scream if I don't put your paper under your doormat.

This time she banged on the top of her window while she yelled, 'Tony Miglione! I know you can hear me!'

Sure I can. So can the whole neighbourhood.

'Don't you forget to put my paper *under* my doormat!'

I didn't say anything.

'TONY . . .'

Then I turned around and looked up at the window. 'Who, me?'

'Yes . . . you!'

'But it's pouring, Mrs Gorsky,' I called.

'So? You won't melt.'

Maybe I will. Then you'll be in big trouble because my family will come looking for me and

1

you'll have to tell them how I melted down to nothing right on your front porch.

I walked away from Mrs Gorsky's house. She was still banging on her window. Well, let her. I didn't feel like climbing her porch steps. What's the worst thing she can do to me? Call my boss . . . that's what. So? He'll understand. There's no rule that says I've got to put the paper under her doormat. As long as it doesn't land in the bushes I'm allowed to throw it from the sidewalk. If this rain ever stops, I'll go back to doing it her way. Then she'll be satisfied.

I don't know what I'll do about my paper route next year, when I go to junior high. I don't want to give it up. But Jefferson Junior has an after-school basketball league and I want to play in it. Basketball is my favourite sport. I just wish I was taller. My brother Ralph says I'll probably sprout up at fourteen like he did. I hope I don't have to wait that long. It's important to be tall when you're playing basketball. You're that much closer to the basket. I play at the Y all day Saturday and every Sunday afternoon. Always with the same bunch of guys – Frankie Bollino, Joe Schenk, Joe Rosella and Billy Turner. We call the two Joes, Big Joe and Little Joe. Rosella's the big one.

Maybe my boss will let me deliver later in the afternoon next year. I hope so. I could get around a lot faster if I had a bike I could depend on. But all

I've got is Ralph's old one, which doesn't work most of the time. I've been thinking about buying a new bike – a ten-speed Schwinn – bright red. But my father says it's more important to put my money in the bank for college. He's saving for my education already and I don't even know what I want to be. Suppose I don't want to go to college? My father will be disappointed. He wants me to be a teacher, like Ralph. And we have a State Teachers College right here in Jersey City. That's where Ralph went and where Angie goes now. She's Ralph's wife. They live upstairs. Between the two of them you'd think they invented education.

I wonder how I'll feel going to the school where my brother teaches. Probably I won't get Ralph anyway. At least I hope I don't. It'll be bad enough when the other kids find out my brother's The Wizard of Seventh Grade Social Studies. Suppose they get ideas and ask me to fix it with Ralph for them to get good marks? What will I do then?

Wait a minute. Maybe I can say I'm no relation to Ralph Miglione, the teacher. We just happen to have the same last name. After all, Jersey City is a big place. Not everybody knows my family. Yeah . . . that's what I'll say. And I'll warn Big Joe, Little Joe, Frankie and Billy in advance. They're my best friends. They can keep a secret.

If only the rain would stop.

I can hear my mother saying when I get home,

'Why didn't you wear your rubbers? Why are they just sitting in the closet?'

Four more houses and I'll be done delivering for the day. Good . . . I'm starving. I wonder what's for supper. Grandma does all the cooking at home. She's my mother's mother and she's really a great cook. Frankie says he'd rather eat at my house than anywhere.

One thing I really like about Frankie is how he treats Grandma. He acts like there's nothing wrong with her. But Grandma can't talk anymore. She had cancer of the larynx two years ago and they had to operate and remove it. She could learn to talk again through a burping method if she was willing. But she's not willing. She moves her lips a lot, like she's talking, but no sound comes out. If she has something really important to tell us she writes it down – always in Italian, which I can't read.

Once I caught Billy and Little Joe fooling around pretending to be my grandmother. They were waving their arms and moving their lips like Grandma does. When they saw me standing there they stopped.

If I hurry I might get home before my mother. Then I can change my shoes and she won't see how wet they are.

I made it. My mother probably got hung up in traffic somewhere. That happens a lot when the weather's bad. She works in Newark, selling under-wear in Ohrbach's. I wonder what it's like watching ladies try on underwear all day? I'd really like to get a look at that!

I took off my shoes in the front hall and hung my raincoat on the hook. My feet were soaked. So were the bottoms of my pants. I sat down on the floor and peeled off my socks. One had a big hole in it. Angie came flying down the stairs then and almost crashed right into me.

'Tony . . . you're absolutely drenched!'

'I know,' I said. 'It's pouring out.'

She started back upstairs. 'I'm going to get a towel to dry off your hair.'

'I can do it myself,' I told her. Angie likes to play mother with me. Sometimes I let her and sometimes I don't. It depends on my mood. My father says Angie has fat legs. I've been looking at her legs a lot lately and I don't think they're too fat. I think they're nice. Maybe some day I'll marry a girl like Angie. Then again, maybe I won't. Maybe I'll never get married.

I went into my room, dried off and changed my clothes. Then I headed for the kitchen. Grandma was tossing a salad. 'I'm home,' I said.

Grandma smiled and offered me an olive. I really like olives. Big Joe says if you eat a lot of them you make out good with the girls when you're older. But that's not why I eat them. I liked them before I ever heard about that. Big Joe knows plenty. He told me and Frankie about wet dreams. I wonder if I'll ever have one?

'What's for supper?' I asked Grandma.

She pointed to the oven.

'Chicken?' I asked.

Grandma shook her head.

'Lamb?'

She shook it again.

'Veal?'

Now Grandma nodded. I play this game with her every night. She likes me to guess what we're having to eat. The only way I can have a conversation with her is if I ask the questions and she answers by moving her head. As far as I know Grandma spends her time doing two things. One is, she cooks. And the other is, she walks to church every single morning. I think she's Father Pissaro's best customer.

When my mother and father got home we all sat down to supper. Ralph and Angie eat with us every night too. I don't think Angie knows how to cook.

Pop told us that starting tomorrow morning he'll be working on an office building downtown. They need a lot of rewiring done. My father's an electrician. He works for a contractor. He's even got his own truck. It says *Vic Miglione* on the door.

Under that there's a picture of a telephone book with *you saw it in the yellow pages* written across.

'Is it a big job?' my mother asked.

'Pretty big,' Pop said. 'Should last about four weeks.'

'Well, that's something,' Mom said.

I was just about finished with my veal cutlet when Ralph pushed his plate away and said, 'Angie went to the doctor today. You might as well know . . . she's pregnant.'

My mother said, 'Ralph . . . Ralph . . .' She shook her head.

My father closed his eyes.

Grandma moved her lips very fast.

Angie jumped up and ran to the bathroom.

I know I shouldn't think about Ralph and Angie the way I do. I know I shouldn't think about what you have to do to get somebody pregnant. But sometimes I just can't help it. He and Angie really do those things. Ralph admitted it. All of a sudden it was very quiet. Did they know what I was thinking? I tried a laugh and said, 'What's everybody so gloomy about? They're married!' I meant this to be a joke but nobody got it.

'Tony . . . Tony . . .' my mother said in her *Ralph . . . Ralph* voice. 'You don't understand.'

'Understand what?' I asked.

Ralph explained. 'We don't have much money,

7

Kid. Angie was supposed to teach for a few years to get us started. We can't afford to have a baby.'

'Oh . . .' I said.

Angie didn't stay in the bathroom long. She came back to the table and sat down. She didn't look so good but she smiled at me.

'Well, you're going to be an uncle, Tony. How does it feel?'

'Oh fine.' What was I supposed to say?

Then Angie looked at Ralph and started to cry again. My mother stood up and put an arm around her. 'It's all right, Angie. We'll help out. Don't worry.'

'How can I not worry?' Angie asked. 'You and Pop have done so much already. The apartment upstairs and our meals and . . .'

My father coughed. 'Listen Angie, you're my family. That baby is going to be my grandson . . .'

'How do you know it's a boy?' my mother asked.

'I know. That's all,' my father said.

'I'm sorry,' Angie told us. 'I wanted to teach. I really did.'

'I know . . . I know . . .' my mother said, as if repeating everything twice meant it wasn't as bad as it sounded.

'At least Angie will be able to finish college and get her degree,' Ralph said.

'That's good.' My father tried to sound happy.

'Maybe I'll give up Ohrbach's and take care of

the baby so Angie can teach anyway,' my mother said. 'Let's wait and see.'

While my mother was talking, Grandma got up and came back with her pad and pencil. She wrote a note and handed it to my mother, who translated:

We'll call him Vinnie.

Vinnie was my other brother. He was killed in Vietnam. My mother got tears in her eyes and she and Grandma touched hands.

Why does everybody think babies are such an expense? They're very small and they hardly eat anything. While I was thinking this Angie ran into the bathroom again. If you ask me she was puking.

As soon as we got up from the table my father went downstairs. He's got a workshop fixed up in the basement and that's where he spends all his free time. He invents things. I don't understand the stuff he does in his workshop so I don't go down much. Neither does Ralph. Vinnie was the one with the scientific mind. At least that's what my family is always saying.

Tonight, when I go to bed, I might think about Vinnie. I do that sometimes so I won't forget him. Or maybe I'll concentrate on getting good enough to shoot thirty baskets a minute.

In a few weeks the weather changed. It was really spring. I knew because my mother sent my winter jacket to the cleaner. She never does that unless she's sure it's going to stay warm. She says changeable weather is sick weather and that I have to wear a winter jacket until the middle of April, like it or not. What she doesn't know is that as soon as I'm out of sight I take off my jacket and carry it around with me.

Once my father finished the job in the office building he started spending more and more time in his basement workshop. A couple of nights he asked Mom to give him a sandwich for supper and he even ate down there. My mother and Ralph are both working at extra jobs. Mom is staying at the store two nights a week and Ralph is selling shoes after school and Saturdays. Every night the family is so pooped out they fall asleep right after supper. The only good thing about this is I get to watch whatever I please on TV.

One morning in the middle of breakfast, my father came into the kitchen wearing his best suit. He was carrying a small metal box. He didn't sit down at the table. He just grabbed a cup of coffee and said goodbye.

'Where's Pop going?' I asked.

'New York,' my mother said.

'What for?'

'Eat your eggs,' my mother said.

'I am eating them,' I told her. 'What's he all dressed up like that for?'

10

'Finish your milk too.'

I got the point. She wasn't going to discuss it with me.

My father put on his best suit for the next three days. He left the house carrying that metal box every morning and he didn't come home until late at night.

Whatever Pop's secret was I felt pretty lousy that they didn't let me in on it. I had a few ideas of my own though.

1 My father is a secret agent. The electrician business is a front. His real spy work is done in the basement workshop. And his information is in that box.

2 My father is in trouble with the Jersey City mob. He has to testify at hearings every day. The secrets are locked in that metal box.

3 My father is sick. He has cancer, like Grandma. He has to go to New York for special treatments. His medicine is in the box.

The more I wondered about Pop the more my stomach started to hurt. Last January I had really bad stomach pains and my mother took me to the doctor. He said it was nothing – that I just shouldn't eat so much roughage. I told him I never ate roughage in my whole life. The doctor laughed

11

and said roughage is lettuce and celery and stuff like that. So now instead of eating salad every night I have it only once or twice a week. I still get a lot of stomach aches. But my mother says it's gas. I don't even tell her about them, anymore. I'm afraid she'll come after me with the castor oil.

At the end of my father's third day out my mother worked late and Pop met her in Newark. I was already in bed by the time they came home. I was reading *Great Basketball Heroes of our Times* and figuring if I got good enough I could get an athletic scholarship to some college and my father wouldn't need the money he was saving for my education. He could use it to pay for the baby instead.

When they came into my room to say goodnight my mother asked me to put my book away and listen carefully because she had something very important to tell me.

'What is it?' I asked.

'You see Tony . . .' she began. Then she looked at my father and said, 'Oh Vic . . . I'm just too excited. You tell him.'

I sat up in bed. This is it! He's going to tell me. At last I'll know the secret. No matter what it is, I won't break down in front of him. I'll tell him it's all right. That I know how these things can happen.

12

'I've made a deal, Tony,' my father said. 'That is, I think I've made a deal.'

So it's a deal, I thought. He's sold out to protect us. That's why my mother's excited.

'Are you listening, Tony?' my father asked.

'Sure Pop.'

'Well, I'll know more tomorrow when the lawyers talk.'

'What lawyers?'

'Sam Ranken, my lawyer, has to meet with the lawyer for J.W. Fullerbach Electronics,' my father said.

I asked my mother, 'What's he talking about?'

'Tony . . . Tony . . .'

Here she goes again, I thought.

'Your father's a genius! An absolute genius! Did you know that, Tony?' She gave my father a juicy kiss and kept talking. 'I always knew it . . . deep down inside I always knew!'

My father? A genius? What's she talking about now? My father's regular. 'I don't get it,' I said.

'Well, Tony . . .' my father began, loosening his tie. 'One of my ideas about electrical cartridges . . . one of the things I've been working on downstairs . . .'

I interrupted. 'You know I don't understand that stuff, Pop.'

'So listen! Maybe this time you'll understand.'

'Okay . . . I'm listening,' I said.

13

My father told me how he took his idea to Mr J.W. Fullerbach. And how he had to see two assistant secretaries, three regular secretaries and a vice-president before he got to see J.W. Fullerbach himself. But it was worth it because Mr Fullerbach likes the electrical cartridges – and my father – and my father's ideas – and he wants all three.

'You're going to work for him?' I asked.

'We'll see,' my father said.

'You're quitting your job with Mr Dalto?'

'We'll see.'

'Oh.'

'This means money, Tony,' my father said. 'It means Ralph and Angie won't have to worry. Can you understand that?'

'Sure, Pop. Sure I understand.' I put my head on the pillow. My mother turned out the light and kissed me on my forehead.

So my father's not a secret agent.

He's not mixed up with the mob.

And he doesn't have cancer.

But what was he talking about? One of his inventions? He really invented something that somebody wants? Is he a genius? And if he is how come it took so long to find out?

My father took the bus to New York every morning for the next week. His regular boss, Mr Dalto, called in the afternoon to find out how

Pop was feeling. That's how I knew my father had reported in sick. I didn't give him away though. I said, 'He's getting better, Mr Dalto. Thank you for calling.'

At the end of the week, when Pop came home from New York, he picked me up and swung me around. Now that's something he never does anymore. I'm much too big.

So I yelled, 'Hey, put me down!'

Then my father picked up my mother and swung *her* around, then my grandmother and Angie but not Ralph. Ralph is bigger than my father. While he was swinging us all around like that he laughed and yelled, 'We're going to be rich . . . rich!'

My mother hollered, 'Vic! Calm down. You're no kid. Think of your heart!'

So Pop made us all sit down on the couch while he stood up in front of us and told us about his deal.

J.W. Fullerbach Electronics is going to manufacture my father's electrical cartridges. And my father is going to manage the plant that's going to do the manufacturing.

'It's one of the Fullerbach plants in Queens,' my father said. 'But now, thanks to Sam Ranken, it's going to be called the Fullerbach–Miglione Engineering Corporation.'

My mother tried that out for size. 'Fullerbach-Miglione . . . Fullerbach-Miglione . . .'

And I thought, Fullerbach-Miglione?

'I get stock in Fullerbach Electronics, with options, of course . . .' my father said, doing a little dance. 'I tell you . . . *we are going to be rich*!'

I don't know anybody rich. Everybody I know is just like me. I wonder what rich is like. It probably means that Ralph and Angie can have a baby every year.

'Angie, let me kiss you!' my father said. 'If it wasn't for that baby you and Ralph are expecting, I'd never have had the guts to try out my electrical cartridges on anybody.'

'Say, Pop,' I said. 'How're you going to get from Jersey City to Queens every day?' That was the part of it I understood.

'I'm not going to, Tony,' my father said.

'You're not?'

'Nope.'

'Well then, what?' I asked.

'I'm going to get from Rosemont to Queens.'

'What's Rosemont?' I asked.

'It's a town in Long Island.'

'You're going to live there?'

'*We're* going to live there!' my father said.

'We are?' I asked.

'That's right!'

16

'All of us?'
'All of us!'

Goodbye Jersey City, I thought.
Goodbye basketball at the Y.
Goodbye Little Joe and Big Joe.
Goodbye Frankie and Billy.
Goodbye Jersey Journal *paper route.*

'What's the matter, Tony?' my mother asked.

'The Kid's excited,' Ralph said. 'Can't you see . . . the Kid's just so excited!'

'And why not?' my mother asked. 'How many kids have a genius for a father!'

I don't cry any more. I'm too old for that baby stuff, which is why I ran for the bathroom and locked myself in. I cried really quiet. Not like Angie who does it so loud everybody knows.

Chapter 2

We all finished the school year in Jersey City but it wasn't the same for me. Because when the guys talked about Jefferson Junior I knew I wouldn't be there. I didn't tell them we might be moving or about my father's new job. I pretended everything was just fine. Then Pop announced that we had a new house. In Rosemont, just like he promised.

On Sunday afternoon we went for a ride to Long Island. On the way my father said, 'You know, Tony, Mr Fullerbach made all the arrangements for our new house.'

'I know,' I said.

'He says Rosemont's a nice place to live.'

'I know. You already told me.'

'And what a coincidence that Father Pissaro's cousin should be a priest there,' my mother said.

We just found out about Father Pissaro's cousin this morning. After church, Pop told him we were moving to Rosemont and he told us about his cousin. So when Pop said we were going there this afternoon, Father Pissaro said he'd call his cousin and we could stop and say hello.

'I'm telling you, Tony, this family's getting lucky,' Pop said. 'I can feel it!'

It doesn't make me feel lucky to know Father

18

Pissaro's cousin is a priest in Rosemont. It's not that I don't like him. It's just that I don't care one way or the other about his family. I'd feel luckier if my father told me Jimmy Connors or Muhammad Ali lives there.

Pop looked over at me. 'Well, what do you say, Tony? Are we getting lucky?'

A passing car tooted its horn at us then. 'Vic!' my mother shouted. 'Keep your eyes on the road.'

'Who's driving?' my father asked. 'You or me?'

'You . . . you . . .' Mom told him. 'All I'm saying is just be careful.'

'I'm always careful! Right, Tony?'

'Right, Pop.'

We have the same conversation every time we go someplace in the truck. My father looks at whoever he's talking to, my mother yells, 'Be careful!' and my father tells her he's always careful. Usually this happens once going and at least once coming home.

In an hour and a half we got to Rosemont. Pop drove us all around. Rosemont is really something! I think I'd be excited about moving there if only I could take my friends with me.

My father and mother kept smiling at each other. 'Our dream come true, Carmella,' Pop said.

'Oh Vic . . . I love it!' my mother told him, squeezing his arm.

Our new house is a big white one with a round

19

driveway right up to the front door. All I could think of was, who's going to cut all that grass? So I said, 'How much land do we have, Pop?'

And my father said, 'Just about an acre.'

'That's a lot of grass.'

'And look how green it is,' my mother said.

'I guess the gardener takes good care of it,' Pop told her. 'And Mr Fullerbach arranged for the same man to work for us.'

Whew – that's a relief. For a minute I thought I'd get stuck cutting it. And if I had to cut all that grass I'd never have time for basketball. That reminds me – now the guys will find out the truth. That I'm moving away. And I feel kind of bad because our team will break up. How can you play with only four guys on a side?

We couldn't go inside our new house because people are still living there. My father said we should be able to move by 20 July. That means I'll have my thirteenth birthday in Rosemont. I wonder what I'll get?

We drove up and down our street a few more times and then went to visit Father Pissaro's cousin. His church is called Saint Joseph's and it's smaller than our church in Jersey City, but a lot more modern. It's made out of brown bricks and the front doors are all glass. The cross doesn't sit on top of the church. It's built right into the front and goes straight up past the roof. There are a lot of tall trees around it and a parking area right behind. My father pulled the truck in there and we got out.

My mother said, 'Wait just a minute, Vic. I want to fix my hair.'

When she was done we walked around to the front of the church and went inside. It was very quiet. Services were over. The priest was expecting us. He came out to greet us right away. He and my father shook hands.

'I'm happy to meet you, Mr Miglione. My cousin called to say you'd be here this afternoon. Welcome to Rosemont.'

'Thank you, Father,' Pop said. 'I'd like you to meet my wife and my youngest son, Tony.'

'Mrs Miglione . . . I know you're going to enjoy living in Rosemont.'

'Thank you, Father,' my mother said.

Then he looked at me. 'Well, Tony . . . how old are you . . . about twelve?'

'Almost thirteen,' I said.

'In junior high?'

'Yes, I'm starting in September.'

'He would be going into eighth grade, Father,' Mom said, 'but he had pneumonia when he was five and the doctor told us not to rush him into school. So he started a year late.'

My mother's always explaining why I'm a little older than the other kids in my class. If you ask me she's worried that people will think I stayed back. I wish she'd stop explaining. I don't think anybody cares.

'We have an active Junior Youth Group here, Tony,' Father Pissaro said. 'I think you'll like our activities. You can join when school starts.'

'Thank you,' I said. I felt funny about calling him Father Pissaro. He doesn't look like his cousin. He's younger and rounder and he has more hair. To keep things straight in my mind I decided to name him Father Pissaro the Second.

On the way back to Jersey City my father told us that J. W. Fullerbach lives on Long Island too, but much farther out. His chauffeur drives him to work every day.

'Is that how it's going to be for us?' I asked.

'Don't be silly, Tony. We're going to be the same as always. Only we'll have a nice house and a new car,' my father said.

'We're buying a car?' I asked.

'Mr Fullerbach will lease one for us. He does that for all his executives.' My father said *executives* really slow so I wouldn't miss it.

'What kind?' I asked.

'What kind of what?'

'Car. What kind of car will we get?'

'Whatever Mr Fullerbach decides,' my father said.

★

I found out the next week. It's a dark green hardtop with stereo speakers. The inside smells like new shoes.

Big Joe, Little Joe, Billy and Frankie came over to see it right away. I let them sit in it and they were really impressed. Nobody we know has a hardtop with stereo speakers.

Frankie asked me could he take over my paper route since I was leaving town. I told him sure I'd fix it with my boss.

'My father says your father hit it big at the races,' Big Joe said. 'That's how come you got the car and all.'

'That's not how come,' I said. 'He invented something.' How could Big Joe's father spread a story like that!

'Yeah? What'd he invent?' Little Joe asked.

'Some electrical cartridges,' I told him.

'What's that?' Billy asked.

'It has to do with using lamps in the middle of a room. This way you don't have to plug anything in and you don't need a cord. You just attach an electrical cartridge.'

'You mean it's a kind of battery?'

'No, not exactly.' I hated to admit I didn't really understand it myself.

'Never mind any electrical cartridges,' Billy said. 'My father says your father's hooked up with the mob. They bought him the car.'

'That's a lie!' I yelled. I couldn't believe these guys. I always thought we were great friends. So why were they carrying on like idiots! 'The car is part of the deal. So's the new house,' I explained. 'My father's got a good lawyer. He arranged it. A good lawyer's pretty important when you're making a deal,' I said, like I knew all about it.

'If your father's so smart how come he never invented anything before?' Big Joe asked.

'He did,' I told him. 'But he didn't try to sell any of his inventions.'

'So how come he did now?' Little Joe asked.

'Because Angie's going to have a kid and we need some money.' I got out of the car and they followed me. I pretended not to care about what they were saying. I told myself the guys just feel bad because I'm moving away. Only Frankie was the same. He told me we'd still be great friends and he'd visit me and I'd visit him and all that.

That night while I was getting ready for bed, Ralph came into my room and said, 'Guess what, Kid?'

'What?'

'Me and Angie are moving to Long Island too.'

'To Rosemont . . . with us?'

Ralph laughed a little. 'We'd love to live in Rosemont, Kid, but who can afford it? We got a little apartment in Queens. It's a nice neighbourhood with plenty of young people.'

'Isn't that pretty far from Jefferson Junior?' I asked.

'I won't be teaching at Jefferson Junior next year.'

'You quit?'

'I've applied for a teaching job in Queens. No point hanging around Jersey City if the whole family's going to Long Island. Besides, Pop wants to sell this house and it's time for me and Angie to be on our own.'

'Oh.' I finished buttoning my pyjamas and made a ball out of my dirty clothes.

'Hey, Kid . . . aren't you glad? Now we'll still be able to see each other all the time.'

'Sure I'm glad,' I said. I didn't tell Ralph I thought he and Angie would stay in Jersey City and I'd come visit them every weekend and maybe play a little basketball at the Y.

We moved on 20 July just like Pop said. The funny thing about moving was, we didn't even need a moving van. And that was what I was looking forward to most. One of those big orange trucks parked outside our house with a dozen men carrying out all our stuff. The reason we didn't need a moving van was we weren't taking anything old with us, except Grandma's pots and pans and my Jefferson Junior High wall pennant. My mother didn't want me to take it.

'It's old,' she said. 'What do you need it for?'

'I like it,' I told her. 'I want to hang it above my bed.'

'You'll get a new one . . . from Rosemont Junior High.'

'I want this one anyway. It used to be . . .' I almost said, 'Vinnie's.' But I caught myself in time and said, 'Ralph's.' We never talk about Vinnie. Everytime somebody mentions his name Mom starts to cry.

'Oh, all right. If it means so much to you, take it,' she said.

Frankie came over to say goodbye again. He told me he got my paper route and I warned him about Mrs Gorsky. 'You've got to put her paper *under* the doormat or she'll call the boss and report you.'

'Okay,' Frankie said. 'I'll remember.' Then he reached into his pocket and came up with a coin. 'This is for you, Tony,' he said, handing it to me.

'Thanks,' I said, taking it.

'It's from England. It's worth about a dollar.'

'Thanks a lot, Frankie. It's really interesting.' I wished I had something for him too. I was still holding my Jefferson Junior wall pennant. I unfolded it. 'I was hoping you'd come over this morning because I wanted to give you this.' I handed it to Frankie.

'Hey . . . thanks a lot, Tony. That's really nice.'

'It used to be Vinnie's.'

'No kidding! That's really something. I didn't know Vinnie went to Jefferson Junior.'

'Yeah . . . he did.'

'I'll hang it over my bed.'

'That's where I had it.'

'Yeah . . . I know.'

My mother called me then. 'Tony . . . hurry up . . . we're ready to go.'

'Well . . . see you, Frankie.'

'Yeah . . . see you, Tony.'

A few trips in the green hardtop – a few more in the old truck – and Goodbye Jersey City . . . Hello Rosemont!

Everything in our Rosemont house is new except the carpeting. The old owners left it in as part of the deal. It's yellow and it's so thick you can lose your shoes in it. My father says my mother bought out Newark, Jersey City and half of New York fixing up the house. But he doesn't mind. He wants her to enjoy herself now that he can afford it.

I have my own room with my own closet and also my own bathroom, which my mother says I'm supposed to keep neat. Grandma has her own bathroom and so do my mother and father. All of these are upstairs. Downstairs I counted two more, which makes a grand total of five bathrooms in one house. In Jersey City we had one. If anybody had an emergency and the bathroom was in use we always ran up to Ralph and Angie's.

My closet has a light in it. I found this out when I opened the closet door. The light went on automatically. When you shut the door it goes out. You don't even have to bother touching a switch or anything. I spent about ten minutes just opening and closing my closet door.

My bedroom is at the opposite side of the house from my mother and father's. Grandma's is in the middle. I have three windows in my room. Two overlook the backyard and one overlooks the side by the garage. I think the reason we have this circular driveway is so you won't get tired walking from the garage to the front door.

From my two back windows I can see my next-door neighbour's yard. It has a big wooden fence all around it. The kind you can't see through at all if you're on the ground. But from my room I can see right over it. That's how I know we might really be rich and my father isn't kidding around. They have a swimming pool! It's rectangular with a statue at one end. There's a diving board and everything!

The thing is, every time I think about us being rich I get scared. I know it's not going to last. I think the money will run out by January. My father used to kid around about if he won the state lottery the money would probably last five months. It's not that I'll mind moving back to Jersey City. It's just that I'll hate to face the guys. Big Joe will probably laugh and tell me he knew it all the time. And then there's Mom and Pop. They'll really be disappointed. They're so excited about living in Rosemont. But there's nothing I can do about it.

Grandma spent the first few days in Rosemont in the kitchen. She opened every cabinet a million times and wrote my mother a whole pad full of notes. Mostly about the stove and oven which she doesn't like because they're electric instead of gas.

My mother kept telling Grandma what a wonderful kitchen it is . . . so modern! And how easy it will be for her to cook now. My grandmother kept shaking her head. So my mother talked louder. She always does that when they disagree. She talks loud, as if Grandma's deaf. Only Grandma's hearing is fine and talking loud doesn't do any good at all.

I found out what happens to garbage in Rosemont. Number one is, we have an automatic disposal built into the sink. All the food scraps go down there and get ground up. Number two is, we have three garbage cans in the ground by the kitchen door. And twice a week the garbage truck comes by and the cans get emptied. Nobody puts their stuff down at the kerb.

The first few mornings we lived there I got up early and rushed outside. So did Grandma. But not for the same reason as me. She walked to Saint Joseph's every day. I wanted to make some friends

29

before school started. That way I won't really be a new kid. I have a whole month to meet the Rosemont guys. That should be plenty of time. I hung around the front of our house waiting for somebody to notice me. It didn't take me long to find out that my new neighbourhood is dead in the summer. I didn't see any kids. Not even little ones.

On my fourth Rosemont morning I met Mrs Hoober, from the swimming pool house. I was walking up and down my driveway counting stones when I saw her open her garage door. I watched her, hoping she would notice me. She did.

'Oh hello,' she said. 'You new?'

'Yes.'

'I'm Mrs Hoober.'

When she said that I noticed she was carrying a pair of brown and white shoes, with spikes.

'What's your name?' she asked me.

'I'm Tony Miglione.'

'Well, hi Tony.' She got into her car and backed it out of the garage. Then she rolled down the window and told me she was on her way to play golf at the country club.

My mother met her later that afternoon and that night she told my father that our next-door neighbour is Diane Hoober and that Mr Hoober is Vice-President of Amilard Drugs. And aren't we lucky to be rubbing shoulders with such people?

Then my mother told me that the reason I

haven't made any friends in four whole days of looking around is because in Rosemont practically all the kids go away to camp in the summer. And that Mrs Hoober has two kids who'll be home the end of August. Mrs Hoober also told Mom that some families have places at the beach and stay away from June to September.

Back in Jersey City we'd have thought you were pretty lucky to get to spend the summer in a place like Rosemont . . . never mind camp and the beach!

A week later I met Mrs Hoober again. She was getting out of her car with a lot of packages. So I ran over and said, 'Want some help?'

She handed me a big box and said, 'Thanks, Tony.'

I carried it to her front door and then she took it from me. 'I see you're having a lot of work done on your house.'

'Us?' I asked. 'No, we're not having anything done. It's perfect the way it is.'

'Well, that's funny. There's a truck parked in your driveway all the time.'

'Oh . . . that's my father's truck. Sometimes he drives to work when my mother needs the car.'

'It belongs to your father?'

'Sure. It even has his name on the door.'

'Oh . . . well, thanks for helping me, Tony.'

31

'That's okay. Bye, Mrs Hoober.'

That night after supper I said, 'You know what, Pop? Mrs Hoober thought we were having a lot of work done on our house just because she saw your truck in the driveway.'

My mother looked at my father. 'She asked you about the truck?' Mom said.

'No. I told her it was Pop's. She didn't ask me anything.'

The next day, my father came home from work driving a new Ford instead of the old truck. He laughed and said, 'What do I need with a truck now?'

My mother said, 'I'm glad you decided that way, Vic. We don't want to start off on the wrong foot here.'

Did he get rid of the truck just because Mrs Hoober thought we were having some work done? That's crazy!

'You know, Tony . . . you can't get anywhere without a car when you live out here,' Pop said. 'Your mother can't even get a quart of milk without driving a couple of miles. And the truck isn't so good on the highway. I'll be much more comfortable now.'

Sometimes I get the feeling my father can read my mind.

Along with the new car Pop brought home a regulation basketball net and professional basketball. He put up the basket on the garage and said I should keep in practice because he expects great things from me. As a basketball player or what? I wondered.

I spent the next few days shooting baskets until my mother told me the noise was making her head hurt and that *thump, thump, thump* all day long was too much for anybody's nerves. Would I please try to find something else to do a few hours a day, she asked.

So I watched the Hoobers' swimming pool from my window. Nobody ever used it. What a waste! Life in Rosemont was not exactly what you would call exciting.

On 5 August I was thirteen years old. I knew we were having roast beef for dinner and that Grandma baked me a birthday cake. But nobody asked me what I wanted. So I figured our new house is supposed to be a kind of birthday present. And anyway, I just got my basketball equipment. Still, a birthday's a birthday! In Jersey City I always got something. Usually a shirt, a game and $5.00 to spend any way I wanted. But if my family wasn't going to mention my thirteenth birthday . . . well, neither was I. I'd pretend to be happy without any presents.

That afternoon my father came home from the plant early. He hustled me off with him in the green hardtop. He drove past the Miracle Mile Shopping Centre to the middle of another town called Belmart.

'I have a surprise for you, Tony,' my father said, backing the car into a space.

'What?' I asked. 'Tell me.'

'If I tell you it's not a surprise.' Pop laughed. 'You'll see soon enough anyway. Come on.'

I jumped out of the car and followed my father.

The surprise turned out to be a brand-new red ten-speed Schwinn. Wow! This was my best birthday ever!

After that I rode my bike around every day. I explored every street in Rosemont. I knew all the stores downtown. I found my junior high. I found the football field. I found the park. I wished it was September.

Chapter 3

Finally Joel Hoober came home from camp. We met right away. It was after supper and my mother was doing the dishes while Grandma sat at the kitchen table shelling pistachio nuts. I was eating them as fast as she was shelling them. My father was dozing in the other room. He doesn't have a basement workshop in our new house. I guess he doesn't need one now that his hobby is his business. When the doorbell rang my mother asked me to get it.

'I'm Joel Hoober,' this boy said, when I opened the front door. He was my height but thinner, with very light hair and an awful lot of it. When mine looks like that my mother tells me it's time to go see the barber.

'Are you Tony?' he asked.

I nodded because I had a mouthful of nuts. When I finished chewing and swallowed them I said, 'Come on in.'

My mother came out of the kitchen drying her hands on her apron.

'Mom, this is Joel Hoober,' I said.

Joel offered his hand to my mother. 'How do you do, Mrs Miglione. I'm happy to meet you.' Joel pronounced our name right. Not everybody does.

A lot of people say Miglion-ie. But the 'e' on the end is silent.

The doorbell woke up my father. He padded into the hallway in his stocking feet. This time when Joel shook hands he said, 'How do you do, *sir*. Glad to meet you.'

I could tell right away that my mother and father were impressed. None of my friends in Jersey City say *sir*. And we don't shake hands every time we say hello to somebody. Are all the guys in Rosemont like this? I hope not. If they are I may not make any friends here. I wish Frankie lived next door instead of this creep.

'Well, let's not stand here in the hall,' my mother said to Joel. 'Come in . . . come in . . .'

Now why did she have to go and do that? Doesn't she think I can pick my own friends?

Joel followed my mother into the kitchen. 'You want some pistachio nuts?' she asked him.

'No thanks,' Joel said. He spotted my grandmother. I could tell Grandma was studying him because she looked up and squinted. Joel offered his hand but Grandma didn't bother to shake it. He started his line about how happy he was to meet her and Grandma laughed, which is really unusual for her. When she laughs her mouth opens but no sound comes out.

'My grandmother can't talk,' I told him. 'She has no larynx.'

Joel gave me a funny look but he didn't say anything. We walked back into the front hall.

'Do you play chess?' he asked.

'No, do you?'

'Yeah. It's a good game. Maybe I'll teach you.'

'Okay,' I said, but I didn't mean it.

Then he said, 'Can you come over for a swim tomorrow?'

'Yeah . . . I'd really like that.' I didn't tell him I'd been watching his pool most of the summer wishing somebody would invite me over to use it.

Before he left, Joel shook hands with my father again. 'Glad to have met you, *sir*,' he said. And then to me, 'See you tomorrow, Tony.'

'Okay,' I said, closing the door behind him. I'd already learned that when the air conditioning's on you've got to keep all the doors and windows closed.

'What a nice boy!' my mother said.

'Some manners!' my father added.

I wonder how long Joel would last in Jersey City. About a week, I figure . . . if he was lucky!

I went to the Hoobers' right after lunch the next day. The pool was heated. It was cooler than a bathtub but not really cold. I was mighty glad I know how to swim. I don't do anything fancy and I don't dive, but I do jump off the board and in the

Hoobers' pool I could swim back and forth twice before running out of breath.

Joel had on this grubby red bathing suit and he has about the knobbiest knees I've ever seen. I felt funny in the new suit my mother bought me this morning. I should have worn my old one.

The chess board was set up on a round umbrella table. Joel seemed really anxious to teach me how to play. I only let him because, after all, it was his swimming pool.

After I was there almost an hour the back door slammed and Joel's sister Lisa came out. She was wearing a bikini and was very suntanned which made her hair look even lighter than Joel's. All I could think of was *Wow!* She was the best-looking girl I've ever seen in person anywhere. She has curves all over. I turned away from the chess board so I could keep watching her.

Lisa climbed onto the diving board and did a perfect swan dive into the water. After four laps of the crawl she stuck her head up and spit out some water.

'Hey Joel,' she called. 'Who's your friend? He's cute. Too bad he's not a little older!' Then she laughed and started to swim again.

I could feel the red climb from the back of my neck where it started, to my ears and then my face. Why do girls always say *cute*? That's such a dumb word. It makes me think of rabbits.

The next time Lisa came up from under the water Joel yelled, 'This is Tony Miglione from next door.'

'Hi . . .' I called.

But she didn't hear because she was underwater again. I sat back in a lounge chair and watched Lisa swim. She did laps – back and forth, back and forth. Sidestroke, backstroke, butterfly – I got dizzy just watching.

'She's sixteen,' Joel said.

I nodded.

'You want a good laugh? Some day I'll show you her diary. I know where she keeps it.'

I looked away from Lisa. 'No kidding!'

'Yeah,' Joel said. 'It's great.'

Then I remembered how I promised my mother that I would be polite to Mrs Hoober. That I would shake hands and everything, just like Joel. 'Is your mother home?' I asked.

'Nah . . . my mother's never home. She plays golf every day unless it rains. Then she shops or plays cards. When she's not on vacation, that is.'

I wondered if that's what my mother was going to do.

'Hey, you want something to eat?' Joel asked.

'Okay.'

Joel shouted at the house. 'Millicent . . . hey Millicent! We're hungry.'

'Who's Millicent?' I asked.

'The maid. Only her name isn't really Millicent. She's got some Spanish name that my mother can't pronounce so when she came to work for us my mother renamed her. She didn't even speak English then. She taught me and Lisa to curse in Spanish.'

'No kidding!' Maybe there's hope for me and Joel after all.

'Hey Millicent!' Joel called again.

'What you want?' a voice answered from inside the house.

'You got any cake?'

'I got. You come get.'

'I can't. I'm all wet,' Joel hollered.

'Okay. I bring. But no crumbs by pool or your father kill me.'

'She's scared of my father,' Joel said. 'A lot of people are. Not me of course. I know how to handle him. It's easy. Just stay out of his way.'

Later, as I sat in my lounge chair eating chocolate cake, drinking cold milk and watching Lisa, I thought – this is really the life!

I spent most of Labour Day weekend at the Hoobers' pool. I learned to play a simple game of chess. Joel said he'd teach me more next time. I saw Mr Hoober once. Lisa called him George. She was swimming around when Mr Hoober came out the back door. She called, 'Hi George!'

Joel poked me and smiled with half of his mouth. I wondered how he did that. I mean when he smiles regular a whole row of teeth shows. But this way only one side of his lip goes up. He must have developed it from watching old gangster movies on TV.

Mr Hoober said, 'I don't like the George business, Lisa. That will be enough. Do you hear me?'

Lisa dove under the water and stood on her hands. I watched her wiggle her toes around.

I found out that Mr Hoober plays golf twice on Sundays and holidays. Once in the morning with the men and once in the afternoon with his wife. And every Sunday night the Hoober family eats supper at the country club. So when Joel and Lisa had to get dressed to go out I went home.

My mother put me through the third degree. Questions – questions – questions. She's driving me nuts! She's a lot more interested in the Hoobers than she is in my father's new job. I can get her really mad if I want to. When she asks me something I answer, 'I don't know.' I've been saying that all weekend. She's about ready to explode.

Ralph and Angie were already at the house for supper. I asked Ralph was he still going to be the world's greatest teacher and he said, 'Sure, Kid.' But he didn't sound so enthusiastic. All he talked about was my father's electrical cartridges, which is pretty funny for a guy who isn't scientific.

The night before school started me and Joel

made arrangements to ride our bikes together every day.

'Your bike is really neat,' he told me.

'It's just like yours,' I said.

'Yeah, but mine's a year older.'

'Well, it's still the same,' I said.

'Yeah . . . I guess so.'

'See you in the morning.'

'Quarter after eight. Don't forget,' Joel said as he walked home.

I told my mother that me and Joel were going to ride to school together.

'I'm so glad you and Joel made friends,' she said. 'He's such a nice boy. With a face like an angel's!'

I don't know what angels *really* look like but I doubt if it's like Joel. Lisa maybe, but not Joel.

I'm kind of glad me and Joel aren't in the same formroom. This way I can get to make some other friends. But there's one thing that bothers me. When you have somebody your age living next door either you wind up great buddies or you don't talk at all. I'm still not sure how it's going to turn out with us.

Junior high isn't as bad as I thought it might be. Once you get used to those bells ringing all the time and going to different rooms for different subjects it's pretty good. You feel a lot older than sixth grade.

Two guys from my formroom are in all my other classes – Marty Endo and Scott Gold. The three of us stick together. That way if we have trouble finding the right classrooms we look stupid as a group instead of three individual stupids.

Joel turned up in my English class, which is the period right before lunch. When the bell rang we went to the cafeteria together. The cafeteria is really neat.

Joel brought his lunch from home. He carried it around with him in a brown bag. But he bought his milk and an apple. I bought the whole school lunch. So did Marty Endo and Scott Gold.

During the first week of school I found out why Joel brings his lunch instead of buying it. He likes some strange sandwiches. Salami, tomato and may-onnaise is his favourite. His second favourite is onion slices on buttered wholewheat bread. Either way you have to keep a safe distance from him after lunch. I think he enjoys breathing hard after he eats – especially on the girls.

One thing I don't like about the cafeteria is the cashiers. They're all ninth graders. You can tell by the way they look and by the way they ignore the seventh graders. To an eighth grader the cashier might say, 'Hi.' But to a seventh grader, nothing! Now that's a real shock after being in sixth grade where you're the boss of the whole school. Next year I plan to treat the new seventh graders the same way.

I joined the Junior Youth Group at church. It meets every Tuesday night from seven to nine. You have to be in seventh or eighth grade to belong. Marty Endo joined too. And a skinny girl named Corky from our formroom. Father Pissaro the Second stopped in during our first meeting to ask how we were getting along. We all said, 'Fine, Father.' Then he smiled and left.

Our Youth Group leader is Ted Gibbons. He's a sophomore at Long Island Community College. He's really tall, wears glasses, and it looks like he's growing a moustache. When he wants our attention he waves his arms around and hollers, 'Simmer down!' Since there are twenty-four of us it takes a long time to get quiet. Ted told us about some of the things we'll be doing this year. The one I like best is, we're going to have our own basketball team.

Corky raised her hand and asked if she could start a cheerleaders club to go along with the basketball team.

Ted said, 'Sure.'

I think Corky looked at me and smiled then. I didn't smile back. I can't stand skinny girls.

All in all me and Marty Endo agreed that Junior Youth Group seems pretty good. Marty's a nice guy. He reminds me of Frankie, only he's really smart in school. He asked me to go to the movies with him next weekend. He said maybe Scott Gold and Joel can come too. I told him that sounded great. Then I remembered I didn't have any spending money. Mom hands me enough for lunch and Ralph brings me all my school supplies, but there's nothing left for extras. In Jersey City I used to keep a little of my paper route money so I never had to ask Pop for a handout. That's what got me thinking maybe I should get a paper route in Rosemont.

So on Sunday night I said, 'I think I'll try to get a new paper route.'

'What are you talking about?' Mom asked. 'You're not getting any paper route!'

'Why not? I've got a great bike.'

'That's crazy,' Mom said. 'Vic . . . tell him that's crazy.'

'Do you miss your old job, Tony?' Pop asked. 'Is that it?'

'Not exactly,' I said. 'But I could use the money.'

'Vic . . . Tony needs an allowance,' my mother said. 'I don't know why I never thought about it.'

'How much do you need?' Pop asked.

'Whatever Joel gets,' my mother said. 'How much, Tony?'

'I don't know what he gets,' I told her.

'Well, find out,' she said. 'You should get the same.'

'How's ten bucks?' Pop asked.

'You mean a week?' I said.

'Can you manage on that, Tony?' Mom asked.

I laughed. 'Well, yeah . . . sure! That's plenty.'

'Good,' Pop said. 'You buy your lunch out of that, but if you need more you come to me. That's what I'm here for.'

'Thanks, Pop.'

'And don't let me hear you talking about a paper route anymore,' my mother added.

Wow! Ten bucks a week. I wonder what Frankie would say?

Every morning when we get to school me and Joel park our bikes in this huge rack. We all have our own locks and keys. I wear my key around my neck on a silver chain so I won't lose it. To tell the truth I don't know how I would manage in Rosemont without my ten-speed bike.

After school on most days I shoot baskets while Joel sits on the grass watching me. He has a stack of paperback books he's working on. What he does is underline certain passages and then paperclip those pages so it's easy to find what he's looking for. He showed me a couple of them one day. They're pretty good. Our gym teacher told us if we start to think about those things we should keep our mind on sports and that will help a lot. He told us about wet dreams too, only he calls them nocturnal emissions. I'm still not sure if I'll ever have one.

When I read Joel's paperbacks I can feel myself get hard. But other times when I'm not even thinking about anything it goes up too. I don't know what to do about that. I mean, if my brain is working right it's supposed to control my whole body. But if I don't have any control over that part of me what good is my brain? It's getting so I don't have anything to say about what goes on. I think that part of me has a mind of its own.

Suppose it decides to go up in school and everybody notices? Or at a Junior Youth Group meeting? What will I do to get it down? I think from now on I'm going to carry a raincoat with me every day. Then, if anything happens I'll have something to put over me in a hurry.

When football season started me and Joel rode our bikes to the high school field every time there was a home game. Lisa is a cheerleader. She wears red boots and a white sweater with a big R on it. I like the way her hair flops around when she's yelling cheers.

Sometimes she talks to us during halftime. It depends on her mood. Other times you'd think we were strangers. One day Lisa really put on the big sister act. She hugged me and Joel together and told the rest of the cheerleaders, 'These are my favourite guys!' I knew it was a big joke between her and her friends but I didn't care. Because she was touching me and it felt good.

Corky goes to every game too. She hangs around Lisa a lot. Joel told me Lisa is teaching Corky how to be a cheerleader. Corky ought to get Lisa to teach her some other things too. Because Corky looks like a fifth grader. You can't even tell if she's a boy or a girl unless she happens to be wearing a skirt, which is practically never. Her hair is cut short and she's really small. She spends a lot of time giggling. I'll bet Lisa never giggled in her whole life!

One afternoon on the way home from the game Joel asked me if I'd go to the store with him. He needed some notebook paper. I said 'Sure Joel.'

We left our bikes up against the side of the store and Joel went straight to the counter where the school supplies were. He bought two packages of wide-ruled three-hole looseleaf paper. He paid the saleslady and took the bag she gave him.

'I'm done,' he said. 'You need anything?'

'No. I've got plenty. Ralph brought me a whole bunch of supplies last week.'

'Okay. Let's go.'

We walked side by side to the front of the store. I couldn't believe it when Joel grabbed three flashlight batteries from a bin and shoved them into his pockets. I saw him do it. He didn't look at me. He didn't even look back to see if anybody in the store noticed. He just kept walking with that funny lopsided smile on his face. I was sure he was kidding around.

But when we got on our bikes and started for home and he still didn't say anything I knew he wasn't kidding. Should I say something? I wondered. Like uh . . . 'I saw you take those batteries, Joel. Who do you think you're fooling!' Maybe I should have, but I didn't.

We rode home without a word. When we got to my driveway Joel said, 'Why don't you sleep over tonight? That'd be great. I'll show you Lisa's diary and everything. And I've been working on some new books too – real good ones. I'll even let you read them.'

'I don't know, Joel,' I said, very unfriendly.

'Come on, Tony.'

'Maybe,' I said.

Joel went to his house and I went to mine. I locked myself up in my bathroom for about thirty minutes. My stomach hurt bad.

Is taking three batteries worse than cheating in arithmetic? Frankie used to cheat in arithmetic all the time in Jersey City. I never reported him. And how about the telephone booth at the Y? We all used to shake it to make change come out. And when it did I always helped myself like the other guys. Is taking three batteries worse than that? Well, what if it is! What am I supposed to do about it – call the police? I suppose I could. I wouldn't have to give them my name or anything. Or I could tell the man in the store about it. But I don't want to. Really, what I want to do is get a look at Lisa's diary.

If I tell on Joel we'll never be able to be friends. Just when things are looking good and I'm feeling settled. It would be bad news to have to start out all over again.

So I told my mother I was going to sleep over at Joel's.

'Who invited you?' Mom asked.

'Joel did.'

'Is it all right with his mother?'

'How should I know?' Why do I have to get permission for every little thing I do? Isn't it enough to tell her where I'm going? Why does she have to make such a big thing out of it?

But she called Mrs Hoober anyway. The last thing I heard her say before she hung up was, 'Well, I guess it's okay if just the maid is home. After all, Vic and I are right next door.'

I went to Joel's after supper. I got there in time to see his mother and father leave for a dance at the country club and then to see Lisa leave with her date, a senior from Rosemont High who looks like

50

a monkey. I wondered why she was wasting her time on him. I wanted to shout, 'Hey Lisa . . . this guy's a creep! Don't go out with him. Stay home with us. You and Joel can watch TV and I'll watch you. Please stay, Lisa . . .'

But she didn't. She gave the monkey a big smile when he helped her on with her coat. She left without even saying goodbye.

Joel and I were on our own. He explained that Millicent was closed up in her room where she has her own TV. Then he checked his watch and said, 'I have to make a phone call. Come on.'

I followed him upstairs. He said, 'I wish I had my own phone, like Lisa. Then I wouldn't have to go into my parents' bedroom all the time.'

I have never seen a bedroom like Mr and Mrs Hoober's. They have a round bed. It's hard to believe anybody really sleeps on it. It's two steps up from the rest of the room and I thought, if you fall out of bed here you also fall down the stairs. I started to laugh. Besides the bed being round there's a lamp hanging over it. If Mr Hoober sits up in bed does he whack his head on it?

Joel jumped up the two steps and sat down on the edge of the bed. He took the phone off the hook, and dialled. He examined his fingernails while he waited for someone to answer. 'Hello,' he finally said. 'Is Denton F. Buchanan in? Oh . . . I'm sorry sir. I'll dial again.'

51

I wondered who Denton F. Buchanan was.

Joel hung up and tried again. 'Hello. May I please speak to Denton F. Buchanan. What? Wrong number . . . the second time? I'm terribly sorry sir.'

He looked up at me and smiled as he dialled again.

'Hey, why don't you check the phone book, Joel,' I suggested.

He dismissed me with a wave of one hand. He got his number. 'Hello . . . Denton F. Buchanan please. Yes, I'm sure this is the number he gave me, sir. Yes . . . well, I do understand. But I have checked with information, sir. Certainly. I won't make the same mistake again.'

'Joel,' I said. 'Will you look it up? Who is he anyway?'

'You'll see,' Joel said. 'This is my last phone call.'

He dialled. 'Hello,' he said, disguising his voice. He made it sound very deep, which isn't exactly easy the way his voice changes around from high to low all the time. 'This is Denton F. Buchanan calling. Have there been any calls for me?'

Then he hung up and rolled around on the bed laughing and holding his sides. 'Isn't that the greatest! That poor guy. He really thought I was serious at first.'

More laughing and rolling around – now tears running down his face. 'Who was he?' I asked.

52

'Who knows! I just made up the number. I always do that.'

'You were fooling around?' I asked. 'You don't know any Denton F. Buchanan?'

'Of course I don't know any Denton F. Buchanan! I don't know any Manfred T. Oliver either.' Joel sat up. 'That's the other name I like to use. You've got to try it. You've got to hear how funny it is at the other end.'

'Now?' I asked. I really didn't want to call anybody. I think you can get into big trouble for fooling around on the phone. But if I refuse Joel will call me chicken.

'You can't call now,' he said. 'I only make one call a night. The next time you're over you can try it. Okay?'

'Sure,' I said. Whew – now he won't know I'm chicken. 'Listen, what about Lisa's diary?' I didn't want to seem too anxious but after all, that was the main reason I decided to accept Joel's invitation to spend the night.

'Oh yeah. I promised, didn't I. Come on.'

I followed Joel to the opposite end of the upstairs hallway. Lisa's room is right next to Millicent's. Joel held a finger over his lips as we tiptoed past her door. Inside Lisa's room Joel snapped on a light and whispered that he's not allowed in there. It's off-limits.

He shut the door. Lisa's bedroom is all pink and

white. Girly-looking. Her room faces the side of my house. I looked out her window and saw my room across the way. My shades were up. The light from our upstairs hallway made it easy to see everything. I'd have to be a lot more careful about pulling down my shades from now on. I wouldn't want Lisa to be able to see me. I hope she doesn't know that's my room.

'Psst . . . give me a hand with this mattress,' Joel whispered. 'She keeps it under here.'

I held up the mattress while Joel searched. But all he came up with was a note. It said:

too bad snooper
your sister's smarter than you think!!!

'How about that!' Joel said. 'She found out and moved it. Well, never mind. We'll find it. It's got to be in here some place.'

He started searching her dresser drawers, then went to her desk, dressing table and finally to her closet. But he couldn't find it anywhere. I could tell he was embarrassed because he promised he'd show it to me and now he couldn't make good on his promise.

'I'm really sorry,' he said.

'Forget it,' I told him. I didn't want him to think I cared much.

Just as Joel was climbing back down from Lisa's

top closet shelf the door opened. It was Millicent. She looked funny. She was wrapped in a plaid blanket and her hair was up in curlers.

'What you doing?' she asked.

'Never mind,' Joel said.

'What never mind! I gonna tell on you, Joel. You no supposed to be in here. This time I gonna tell.'

Joel shook his finger at her. 'Will you listen to that!' he said to me. 'Is she a good one? You tell on me, Millicent. You go ahead. Then I'll tell on you!' Joel shouted.

'What you mean?' Millicent asked.

'You know,' Joel said.

I didn't much like him having a fight with Millicent in front of me. I don't think you're supposed to talk to somebody who works for you like that.

'Oh . . . you give me hard time, Joel. But some day God gonna punish you! *You wait.*' Millicent crossed herself and left. I heard her slam the door to her bedroom.

Joel turned out Lisa's light and we went back to his room. 'How do you know she's not going to tell on you?' I asked.

'She wouldn't dare!' Joel laughed. 'She's scared of me! I caught her trying on my mother's clothes one night. If I tell my mother she'll lose her job. And she knows it!'

I'm beginning to change my mind about Joel.

He's not the kind of creep I thought he was when I first met him. He might last longer than a week in Jersey City after all. But the more I know about him the more I'm not sure if I want to be his friend.

Chapter 4

On 19 October Angie had a baby girl. My father was disappointed. 'A first baby and it's a girl! There hasn't been a girl born first in my family for five generations!'

'So what?' my mother said. 'A girl's just as good. Anyway, I always wanted a daughter. Now I have a granddaughter!'

They named the baby Vincenza, after my brother Vinnie – just like Grandma planned. But everybody is supposed to call her Vicki for short. Lucky for her – who'd want to go through life with a name like Vincenza?

When Angie came home from the hospital we all went to Queens to visit the new baby. My mother said she was the most beautiful thing she'd ever seen in her whole life. I thought the baby looked like a plucked chicken, but I didn't say so.

Grandma stood over Vicki making funny faces but all Vicki did was cry. Then the baby-nurse, Mrs Buttfield told us we'd better not stay long because new mothers and new babies shouldn't have too much company right away. She said this like she owned Vicki.

Mrs Buttfield is a present from my mother to Angie. My mother wants Angie to rest and not have to get up at night with the baby. Privately, I renamed the nurse The Butt. She looks about eighty and I know she doesn't want anybody hanging around.

Ralph pranced through the apartment with a big box of cigars. He even offered one to me.

'Go on, Kid, take it. You're an uncle now.'

'What, are you crazy?' my mother yelled at Ralph. 'He's thirteen years old. A cigar! You want him to wind up in the hospital?'

My mother didn't have to worry. I wasn't about to smoke one. Cigars stink!

All afternoon I kept thinking, I could be home playing basketball instead of wasting my time in a stuffy apartment in Queens. It's really funny, the way everyone is so excited about a baby that looks like a plucked chicken. Maybe Vicki will get better-looking. Then again, maybe she won't. Maybe she will always look like that. I feel sorry for her. But why should I worry? She's not my kid. Right?

When we got ready to go home I told Ralph and Angie that Vicki is really neat and very pretty too. That's what everyone else was saying so I decided to be polite about the whole thing. Sometimes it's better to tell a little lie than to tell the truth and have everybody hate you.

When Angie said goodbye she called me Uncle

Tony and she kissed my cheek. I only let her because she just had a baby.

The next Sunday, when Mom and Pop got ready to go to Queens I said, 'I'm staying with Joel this afternoon. We might go to the movies.'

But the Sunday after that when I tried the same thing Mom asked, 'How do you think Ralph and Angie feel that you don't want to see Vicki? Very bad, I'll tell you that. And you're her only uncle too.'

'Oh . . . all right. I'll go with you today.'

When we got there The Butt wanted to check my hands before I even *saw* the baby. Clean hands and runny noses are the big things in Mrs Buttfield's life. I was about to tell her I wasn't interested in touching Vicki and that I was only looking to be polite.

But Ralph said he'd had enough of her and her inspections. So The Butt packed her bags and left. This made Angie cry for a long time and say she didn't know how she was going to manage all by herself.

A week later my mother started the maid business at home.

'I can't run this big house with no help, Vic. I want to enjoy my granddaughter. I don't want to be stuck here all day cleaning the place.'

My father was behind his newspaper and I

couldn't tell if he was really listening until he said, 'So get some help, Carmella.' He spoke without taking his cigar out of his mouth.

'You mean it, Vic?' my mother asked.

'Of course I mean it. I wouldn't say it if I didn't mean it, would I?'

The next day my mother drove to an employment agency and came home with our first maid. She was from South America, her name was Gerta, and she spoke only Spanish. I thought about Millicent and wondered if Gerta would teach me to curse in Spanish.

After five days my mother whispered to my father, 'If I look at her wrong she cries. I think she's very lonesome. I hope she'll improve with experience.'

My father said, 'I'm sorry if she's lonesome. But I can't wear my shirts with wrinkles down the front.'

'I can't tell her, Vic. She'll cry.'

'Then I'll tell her,' my father said.

That was the end of Gerta.

The next week my mother came home with Vera. She was from Haiti and spoke only French.

My father said, 'Why can't you get one that talks Italian?'

My mother said, 'Oh Vic!'

But after a few days my mother complained that Vera didn't like to get up in the mornings and my father complained about the way the beds were made.

That was the end of Vera.

Pauline, LaBelle and Florie followed. Grandma took care of them. Even though she can't talk she can just *look* at you and you know what she's thinking. And she wasn't thinking anything good about any of our maids.

Then Maxine arrived. You could tell she was different right away. First, because she interviewed my mother instead of my mother interviewing her. When she saw me she said, 'When I wash the floor nobody walks on it. That includes you. Understand?'

My mother said, 'Tony's a good boy. You won't have any trouble with him.'

'He'll stay out of my way?' Maxine asked.

I thought, who'd want to get in your way?

My mother put her arm around me. 'Of course he'll stay out of your way. Won't you, Tony?'

'Sure, sure,' I said. I wonder if she'll try on my mother's clothes, like Millicent. I don't think so. She's about a foot taller than my mother.

'Well . . .' Maxine said, running her finger along the furniture, then inspecting it for dirt, 'I'll try it.'

My mother sighed with relief and later she told us that Maxine has excellent references and we are to do everything possible to keep her happy. This included all new towels for Maxine's bathroom. In her favourite colours – purple and brown.

On Maxine's third day she told my mother that *she* had to be in charge of the kitchen. Not the *old lady.*

My mother said, 'Oh dear! I just don't know about that.'

Maxine tapped her foot at my mother.

'You see,' my mother explained, 'Mama's always done all the cooking.'

Maxine glared.

My mother tried a nervous smile. 'I suppose we could arrange something. I mean, why should Mama work so hard when she doesn't have to?'

I thought, Grandma's going to be furious when she hears about this.

She was furious all right. She stomped to her room, slammed the door and refused to come out. My mother banged on her door and called, 'Please, Mama! You'll take it easy for a change. You'll enjoy it . . . I know you will. Just let me explain.'

But Grandma wouldn't open up. Maxine was in charge now and Grandma knew it. There are times when I'd like to throw something at my mother. How can she let Maxine boss her around? Doesn't she care about Grandma? Can't she see how she's hurt her feelings?

The next night my father brought home a colour TV for Grandma's room. Lately, my mother and father seem to think that presents can fix everything. And if you ask me, they think more about Maxine than they do about Grandma.

Every night during dinner my father says, 'Delicious, Maxine!' Of course Maxine stands over him until he says it. After our meal my mother says, 'Thank you very much, Maxine.' Like she's doing us some kind of favour!

When Grandma did the cooking nobody paid much attention to it. And it was better than Maxine's, I'll tell you that. Maybe not as fancy-looking, but better tasting. Since Grandma won't eat anything that Maxine cooks my mother fixes her meals separately. Usually Grandma gets a broiled lamb chop for supper – on a tray in her room. Grandma won't come downstairs any more. She never even goes to church.

One night I walked into the kitchen while Maxine was cleaning up. I saw her throw away all the leftovers.

'Well, Mr Big Eyes,' Maxine said. 'What do you want?'

'How come you're throwing all that food away?' I asked.

'Who's going to eat it, do you think?'

I thought, in Jersey City we saved everything – including cold spaghetti! I made up my mind right then to study extra hard. The way my mother and father are throwing money around I figure there won't be anything left by the time I'm ready for college. If I decide to go I'll need a full scholarship.

I bought a small chess set with some of my allowance. Not a fancy one like Joel's, but the pieces are made of wood. I taught my father how to play.

Pop's not as tired out as he used to be. Business at the plant is okay and things are running smoothly. Every night after supper we sit in the den and play a game. Pop says chess is good because it teaches you how to solve problems. He likes it so much he keeps on playing even after I have to go up to my room to do my homework. He has a make-believe opponent he calls Sam. Pop moves the pieces for both of them. Sometimes I think he likes playing with Sam better than me.

We were in the middle of a hot game one night when the doorbell rang. It was Father Pissaro the Second.

'Vic!' my mother called. 'Look who's here.'

Pop stood up. 'Father . . . what a surprise!' He looked at my mother as if to say, *Did you invite him without telling me?*

And my mother looked back at him with a *don't ask me* expression on her face.

So I said, 'How come you came to see us, Father?'

'Tony!' my mother said. 'Where are your manners?'

64

Father Pissaro the Second smiled at me. 'That's all right, Tony. I really came to see your grandmother. I've missed her.'

My mother took a big breath. Then she smiled. 'Oh Father . . . that's very nice of you. Mama hasn't been feeling too well.'

'I'm sorry to hear that,' Father Pissaro said. 'Do you think I could see her? I know she'll want to make her confession. She never used to miss a week.'

'Well, Father, that's very thoughtful of you,' my mother said. 'Would you give me a minute to run upstairs and tell Mama you're here?'

'Take your time, Mrs Miglione,' Father Pissaro said.

I wondered if Grandma would make a fuss. And how does she confess every week when she can't talk? Does she write it all down or what?

'How's the Junior Youth Group going, Tony?' Father Pissaro asked.

'I like it a lot,' I said. 'Ted is really nice.'

'How about a drink, Father?' Pop asked.

'No thank you.'

'Coffee, or tea?' my father said. 'It's no trouble.'

'Thank you Mr Miglione, but I really don't want anything.'

We looked at each other for a while and then my mother called from the top of the stairs. 'You can

65

come up now, Father. Mama would like to see you.'

After she showed Father Pissaro to Grandma's room, my mother came downstairs. 'I hope Mama doesn't tell him anything to embarrass us,' she whispered to my father.

'She has a right to tell him whatever's on her mind,' Pop answered.

'But you know how stubborn Mama can be these days. She might tell him something just to get back at me.'

'For what, Carmella? She's not a prisoner here. She can come out of her room any time she feels like it.'

'Shush . . .' my mother whispered. 'Here he comes.'

That didn't take long, I thought. Did Grandma tell him any family secrets? I studied his face. But I couldn't tell anything from his expression. It was the same as before. Still, I don't think it would be easy to fool Father Pissaro the Second.

After he left my mother ran up to Grandma's room. She knocked and knocked but she couldn't get in. Grandma had locked her door again.

This morning, before I left for school, my mother said, 'I think it's pretty funny that a boy who won't wear rubbers when it's pouring out suddenly carries an old raincoat around with him every day.'

'I like my raincoat,' I said. 'It's comfortable.' I wasn't about to explain the real reason I took it to school.

'You have a new jacket,' Mom said. 'I'd like to see you wear it once or twice before it's outgrown.'

'Maybe I'll wear the jacket tomorrow.'

'Maybe you'll wear it today!' Mom held the jacket and shook it at me. 'Put it on, Tony, and leave that old raincoat home. It doesn't look nice for school. Besides, it's sunny out.'

'Oh . . . okay.' If I made a big scene she might get suspicious.

So I wore the new jacket to school and worried all day about what might happen. But nothing happened. Maybe it's a question of mind over matter.

One Friday in November, right after second period, I met Joel in the boys' room. He was up on the sinks singing, 'There was a girl in our town – her name was Nancy Brown . . .' When he saw me he yelled, 'Hey Tony . . . watch this!' So I stood there and watched as Joel ran up the row of sinks, then down it. By that time he had quite an audience and of course nobody could wash his hands. I wished my mother could have seen the Angel. As Joel sang his voice cracked. Everybody cheered. When the second bell rang Joel jumped down from the sinks and went to his class.

That day at lunch Joel was in front of me on line

in the cafeteria. He still buys his milk and apple every day. Always the same routine. But this time I saw him take his apple, inspect it for bruises like usual, then stick it into his brown lunch bag. He only paid for his milk. I really got mad when I saw that.

After five days of watching Joel do this I wanted to shout at the cashier, 'Hey, this guy's stealing apples!' I'd yank it out of his lunch bag and shove it in the cashier's face. 'You see,' I'd say. 'You see how stupid you are – even if you are in ninth grade! He's been doing it for a week – stealing an apple a day for a week – and you haven't even noticed!'

Then I figured the cashier would look up at me and say, 'Please tell me what to do.' And I'd tell her in this deep voice, 'Call the principal, stupid!' Then the principal would pat me on the back and tell me, 'What we need is more young men like you, Mr Miglione. Honest – brave – unafraid young men!'

But Joel would never speak to me again. Marty Endo and Scott Gold would call me Snitch. So what did I do about the whole situation? Nothing! As usual.

I paid the cashier and carried my tray of meatloaf and mashed potatoes to our regular table. I sat down between Joel and Marty Endo. As I began to eat I got an awful pain. *Wow!* It nearly doubled me over.

68

'What's the matter?' Joel asked.

'I don't know,' I said. 'I got a pain in my stomach.'

'You want to go to the nurse?'

'No, I think it's going away.' After a few minutes it disappeared and I ate some of my lunch but I didn't enjoy it.

The pain came back that night after dinner and I went to my room to rest. That's when I discovered I could see Lisa's room from my room. I don't know why I never thought of it before. I guess I've been so busy pulling down my shades to make sure she can't see me it never entered my mind that I could see her. With all my lights turned off and with her lights turned on, I can see everything she's doing. And what she was doing was getting undressed. I forgot about my pain and concentrated on my window.

Chapter 5

There was no school on Veterans Day. Just as we were finishing breakfast Grandma walked into the kitchen. She was dressed in black. All three of us stopped eating. This was the first time she'd come out of her room since Maxine started running things. Grandma handed my mother a note. First my mother read it to herself. Then she jumped up and hugged Grandma.

'Oh Mama . . . you remembered!' My mother read us the note:

I'm ready to go to the cemetery.

I thought we wouldn't go this year. Somehow I figured that we've changed so much since coming to Rosemont we'd be able to skip the cemetery deal. But no, we were going. We go every year on Veterans Day, to bring flowers to Vinnie's grave. He's buried in Perth Amboy, which wasn't a bad trip from Jersey City.

From Rosemont it takes forever. We were all squeezed into the car. Me, my mother and my father in the front. Grandma, Ralph, Angie and the baby in the back. My mother kept turning around to talk to Ralph and Angie.

70

'If only Vinnie could see her. He'd be so proud! If only he knew he had such an adorable little niece.' My mother sniffled and I knew what was coming. Every year she devotes the whole day to talking and crying and saying if *only* about Vinnie. I always feel like an outsider on Veterans Day.

On the way to Perth Amboy Angie had to feed the baby. Halfway through her bottle Vicki spit up. It landed on Ralph. So Ralph passed Vicki to Grandma while Angie tried to clean off his jacket. After Vicki finished her bottle she started to cry. My mother said she must have gas. So Grandma passed Vicki to my mother in the front seat so she could try to burp her.

When Vicki cries her face turns bright red and she looks like she's going to explode. Finally Angie handed my mother a pacifier for Vicki to suck. I'm glad we don't have a baby at home. Two hours in the car is enough.

When we got to Perth Amboy my father tried to find the same florist as last year. My mother argued with him about that.

'What's the difference? One florist is as good as another.'

But my father said, 'I remember him. He was a nice guy. He went out of his way to be nice.'

'So you'll waste the whole day looking for him!' my mother snapped.

This went on for twenty minutes. Finally my

father found the florist he was looking for. We all got out of the car to stretch our legs. My mother and Angie talked on and on about what kind of flowers to buy this year. Grandma kept pointing to yellow chrysanthemums but my mother said they reminded her of football games and that she preferred something all white, in a graveyard container.

We piled back into the car with me holding this huge arrangement of flowers. Last year it was only a third as big.

When we got to the cemetery I carried the flowers to Vinnie's grave and stuck the container into the ground. I stepped back and brushed off my hands. My mother bent down and sort of fluffed out the flowers. Then she cried. 'Oh Vinnie . . . Vinnie . . . I miss you so much,' she said. She covered her face with her hands.

Grandma kneeled and kissed the grave. She does that every year. It makes me feel awful. I hate it. Why can't I feel the way they do? Why can't I remember things about Vinnie and cry too? My father just stared at the grave and rocked back and forth on his feet. Angie held the baby close and whispered to her. She's telling Vicki about Vinnie, I thought. About how he died for his country and all that. About how brave he was and how he understood everything my father did in the basement in Jersey City.

Does Vinnie know about us now? Does he know that we live in a big white house and that we drove here in a new green hardtop instead of the old truck? Does he know that Grandma has her own colour TV because she's not allowed to cook anymore? Does he know about our boss, Maxine? And if he knows, what does he think? Is he laughing at us? Is he laughing and saying, 'Hey, what happened to you guys since you visited me last year?'

Ted Gibbons organized our Junior Youth Group basketball team. He said anybody who wants to play *can* play. He told us he remembers what it's like to try out for a team and not make it. So we wound up having two teams. Only two guys in our Youth Group didn't want to play and one of them agreed to be Ted's assistant coach and the other one said he'd like to be our sports reporter.

Ted meets with us every Friday afternoon at our junior high. We don't have any after-school activities on Friday so Ted got permission from the principal for us to use the gym. Ted's moustache is getting thicker. He touches it a lot as if he's checking to make sure it's still there. He's worked out a whole schedule of games for us. We're going to play every Friday night during January and February. Eight games in all against teams from other churches and temples. Since we have two teams

Ted said we'll alternate and change over at every halftime. That way we'll all have a chance to play.

We started our practice right before Thanksgiving. I'm the best foul shooter. And I'm fast too. I think Ted is pretty impressed. I just wish I was taller. Because when somebody like Marty Endo guards me I can't shoot at all. I can't even see!

When I'm playing basketball I don't think of anything else. Not Lisa or school work or my family. I concentrate on the ball and getting it into the basket. Basketball makes me feel good. I wish we didn't have two teams. I wish I could be in there all the time.

The whole family was invited for Thanksgiving. My three aunts and uncles and my cousin Ginger from Weehawken. Ginger belongs to my mother's sister Rosemary. We call her Aunt Rose. Aunt Rose is married to Uncle Lou. Uncle Lou's Jewish and my mother doesn't approve of him. It has nothing to do with him being Jewish she says. It's just that he isn't *right* for Aunt Rose, which is pretty funny because they've been married for fifteen years.

This was the family's first visit to Rosemont and my mother was really doing it up big. She hired another lady to help Maxine in the kitchen so Maxine wouldn't get all tired out what with cooking the turkey and all. Grandma refused to join us. She hasn't left her room since Veterans Day.

My mother begged, 'Please, Mama . . . just this once! It's Thanksgiving. Give me some pleasure, Mama! Get dressed and come downstairs. *Mama* . . . will you please turn off that television set and come down for dinner!' But Grandma wouldn't budge.

Angie brought Vicki in a car bed. She was supposed to sleep in it all afternoon but nobody told *her* that because she screamed a lot. So we played Pass the Baby. All my aunts and uncles got to hold her and make silly faces at her until my mother came up with the brilliant solution of leaving Vicki upstairs with Grandma while we ate.

Angie took the baby to Grandma's room and then even if she was screaming we couldn't hear her. A very important thing to remember about babies is that if you can't hear them they're not so bad.

My relatives were really impressed with Rosemont and our house. Uncle Lou kept telling Ginger, 'Now you can say you have rich relatives, baby. *Really* rich relatives!'

And Aunt Rose said, 'When Ginger gets older Tony can fix her up on dates and she can sleep over here.'

'Oh, can I, Aunt Carmella?' Ginger asked.

My mother nodded and smiled.

I thought, I'll never fix you up Ginger, because you're dumb and ugly and I don't like you anyway!

Uncle Lou said, 'Rose thinks of everything, doesn't she? Why should Ginger go out with a poor boy if she can go out with a rich one, right?'

So I said, 'What's so great about being rich? Money isn't everything, you know.'

They all laughed. Even Ralph and Angie laughed. Ralph said, 'Listen, Big Shot . . . wait until *you* have to pay for baby shoes!'

How does he know so much about baby shoes? I wondered. Vicki doesn't even wear shoes yet! Ralph is different lately. He isn't The Wizard any more. He's just like an old guy with a wife and kid. Would he be like this if we were still in Jersey City? Is it being a father that changed him?

Finally we sat down to dinner. I've never eaten so much in my life. For dessert we had a choice of three pies – pumpkin, apple or lemon meringue. I chose lemon meringue because I knew Angie baked it and Maxine baked the other two.

After dinner the family went upstairs one at a time, to visit with Grandma.

When Aunt Rose came downstairs she said, 'Mama's lucky to be able to spend her last years in such luxury.'

'And with her own colour TV,' Ginger said.

Later they all decided the reason Grandma 'took

to her room' was plain old age. I could have told them the truth but I'd have got in a lot of trouble.

My father offered Ralph and my uncles cigars. He laughed as he told them each one cost $1.00. When they all lit up, Aunt Rose asked Ginger to recite for us. Ginger's been doing that ever since I can remember. You'd think by now she'd know how dumb she sounds. You'd think she'd be too embarrassed to stand up in front of a bunch of relatives and say her stupid poems. But no! She jumped right up and started.

She had some new poems this year. Two about Thanksgiving, naturally, and one about *love* by Elizabeth Barrett Browning. When she recited that one she closed her eyes. How I wished Joel could have heard her!

When Ginger was through I heard Aunt Rose telling my mother that Ginger wears a bra already, which reminded me of Lisa. Soon it will be dark outside and I'll be able to watch her from my window. When I feel my neck turn red hot I know I better think about basketball in a hurry.

Corky's real name is Kathryn Thomas. I found out because a girl in my formroom named Marian passed me a note. It said:

K. T. thinks T.M. is super!

I knew who T.M. was . . . me. But I didn't know

who K.T. was. And I really didn't care. So I crumpled up the note and threw it away. I made a disgusted face at Marian. That afternoon I got another note. This one said:

My real name is Kathryn Thomas. Love, Corky

I crumpled up that note too. I wished she'd leave me alone. She's a real pain!

Ever since that day Marian runs over to me every morning and says, 'Hi Tony. How's Corky?'

Corky is always stationed right near us so she doesn't miss a thing.

I answer Marian with a straight face. 'I don't know,' I say. 'Why don't you ask her yourself?'

Then Corky and Marian giggle like crazy until Mrs O'Leary looks up and tells them to settle down.

Marty Endo told me that Corky offered to do his maths homework for a week if he arranged for me to wind up sitting next to her at our Junior Youth Group meetings. Marty wouldn't do it. Why should he? He's great at maths.

The more Corky bothers me the more I think about Lisa. I wish it was Lisa who passed me notes and wanted to sit next to me.

This morning, in maths class, I wasn't thinking about Lisa. I was concentrating on a problem in my book and Miss Tobin called on me. She asked me to go up to the board and show the class how I worked it out.

Just as I finished writing the figures on the board I started to get hard. Mind over matter . . . mind over matter, I told myself. But still it went up. I kept my back to the class and prayed for it to go down.

Miss Tobin said, 'That's an interesting way to solve the problem, Tony.'

For a minute I thought she meant my *real* problem, but then I realized she was talking about the *maths* problem.

'Could you explain your reasoning to the class, Tony?'

I started talking but I didn't turn around. I could just picture facing the class. Everybody would laugh and point to my pants. I wished I was wearing my raincoat.

'We'd hear better if you'd turn around,' Miss Tobin said.

What could I do? Pretend to be sick and run out of the room? Maybe. Or just refuse to turn around? No. Ask to go to the bathroom? No . . .

'Tony . . .' Miss Tobin said.

'Yes?'

'We're waiting for you to explain the problem.'

'Oh. Okay, Miss Tobin.'

I was holding my maths book in my left hand and a piece of chalk in my right. I turned sideways, keeping my book in front of my pants. I explained my answer as fast as I could and Miss Tobin didn't ask me any questions. She said, 'Thank you, Tony. You can sit down now.'

I walked back to my seat still holding the maths book close to me. But I didn't have to worry. By then it was down.

From now on I'm going to make sure I always have a stack of books with me. Books are a lot better than my old raincoat!

One afternoon after Thanksgiving vacation Joel came over. My mother was in Queens with Angie and Vicki as usual and Grandma was locked in her room. So was Maxine. She has this strict rule about how she has to have an afternoon nap every day, so she'll be fresh as a daisy for supper, she says. My mother says, of course that's only fair. So we're not supposed to disturb Maxine between three and four-thirty.

While I was pouring two glasses of milk Joel asked if he could use the phone.

'Sure,' I said. I didn't pay any attention until I heard him ask for Denton F. Buchanan. I thought, oh no! He's at it again.

He dialled two more times, going through his whole routine, before he called back and said, 'This is Denton F. Buchanan. Have there been any calls for me?'

I said, 'Same old tricks!'

Joel said, 'Why don't you try it?'

'No. I don't think so.'

'Come on, Tony! Make up the name yourself.'

'I don't know, Joel. I could get in trouble.'

'For what? Nobody's going to know. Come on . . . think up a good name. You're not chicken are you?'

'No.'

'Well then . . . go ahead.'

'Oh . . . all right.' I concentrated until I came up with a name. 'How's Peter Ira Grinch?' I asked.

'Peter Ira Grinch? That's a nutty name.'

'I suppose . . . but it has good initials,' I said.

'P. I. G. Hey, yeah! I like that,' Joel said.

'How do I do it?'

'Just dial a number. Make sure it's not long distance though.'

I picked up the phone, clearing my throat several times as I dialled seven digits and waited. It rang twice before a lady answered.

'Hello,' she said.

'Uh . . . hello. May I please speak to uh . . . Peter Ira Grinch.'

'What number you calling?'

I repeated the number I dialled.

'You got the right number but nobody's here by that name.'

I hung up.

81

'You did fine,' Joel said.

'I did?'

'Sure. Now call back.'

I dialled.

This time she answered right away. 'Hello.'

'Peter Ira Grinch, please.'

'Look kid . . .' How did she know I was a kid? 'I told you . . . you got the *wrong number*!'

I hung up without saying anything. I told Joel, 'She doesn't like me.'

'She doesn't have to like you,' Joel said. 'She doesn't even know you. Go ahead, Tony . . . one more time.'

My hand shook as I dialled. It didn't even ring once.

'Hello,' she said. You could tell she was mad.

'Peter Ira Grinch, please.'

'Listen, you lousy kids,' she screamed. 'I'm fed up with you and your lousy phone calls. I'm gonna call the cops! You hear me? *The cops*. They'll find you and lock you up where you belong!' She slammed the phone down.

'She said she's going to call the cops,' I told Joel.

He laughed. 'She's not calling anybody. Go on . . . call one more time.'

'I can't.'

'What do you mean you can't? You've got to call and say you're Peter Ira Grinch. Otherwise it was all for nothing.'

'I can't,' I said again. 'Don't you know they can trace calls? Don't you know that, Joel?'

'You've got to call her again, Tony!'

I got a stomach pain then. A bad one. 'I can't . . . I can't because I'm sick!' I said, holding my stomach. 'You might as well go home, Joel – I mean it, I'm really sick!' I rushed to the bathroom.

When my mother came home I was still in the bathroom and my stomach was killing me. My mother said nobody can have that much gas and that she was going to take me to the doctor.

She made a lot of phone calls to find out which doctor to see on Long Island. Finally she decided on the one Diane Hoober recommended. My mother thinks everything the Hoobers do is perfect. I wanted to tell her the truth about Joel. I wanted to see how her face would look then, but the more I thought about telling her the more my stomach hurt.

The doctor's name was Frank Holland. He has grey hair and a big nose. He asked my mother to wait in the outer office while he checked me. I had to lie down on his examining table with most of my clothes off while he pushed and prodded at my belly. I was supposed to tell him if it hurt in any special place. It didn't.

'I think we'd better do a test on you, Tony,' Dr Holland said. 'Come back tomorrow morning at eight. Don't eat after six o'clock tonight. And no breakfast in the morning.'

'What kind of test?' I asked.

'Oh . . . I'm going to have a look inside you. It won't hurt. I promise.'

I couldn't sleep at all that night. I was worried about the test and about what might be wrong with me. I hope I don't need an operation. I'm really scared about somebody cutting into me.

The next morning my mother took me back to Dr Holland's office. He was right about the test. It didn't hurt. But he forgot to tell me I'd have to drink a glass of this horrible stuff called barium. It tasted like chocolate-flavoured chalk. Dr Holland explained that when I drank the barium and stood in front of his machine, he could see inside me.

Being a doctor must be really neat. Maybe I'll go to medical school so I can look inside people too. Then again, maybe I won't. Doctors have to do a lot messier stuff than that and I don't even like dissecting frogs in biology.

After the test, Dr Holland said I should get dressed and come into his office. He talked to me from behind his desk. I noticed he doodled on a prescription pad – dog and cat faces mostly. I sat in a chair to his left and I was pretty nervous. My hands were sweating like crazy.

'Well, Tony,' he said, 'there's nothing for you to

worry about. Everything is going to be fine. Your test was normal.'

'I don't need an operation?' I asked.

'No, nothing like that,' Dr Holland said.

'Then what? I mean, why do I get so many pains?'

'Well . . . I think you're pretty tense, Tony. And when a person gets tense about things his insides tighten up and that can cause pain.'

I rubbed my hands on my pants.

'You know, it's nothing to be ashamed of,' Dr Holland said. 'We all face some problems. It's just a question of learning how to handle those problems.'

'Really? That's what it really is?'

'Yes. Some people call it nervous stomach.'

'Oh that. I knew a kid in Jersey City with nervous stomach. He was a creep.'

'Well . . . we hold things inside of us that might be better out in the open. Don't push yourself, Tony. Try to relax and unwind.'

'I am relaxed,' I said.

'Maybe now . . . but not always. In any event I'm going to prescribe some pills for you. One tablet twice a day for two weeks. After that, only when you need them. When you get pains or diarrhoea.'

Dr Holland handed me the prescription.

As I stood up to leave he said, 'What about girls?'

I sat back down. 'Girls?' I asked.

'Yes. Do you think about them a lot?'

'Not much,' I mumbled, looking down.

'It's perfectly normal, you know.'

'Oh sure. I know.'

'Do you like a special one?'

'Kind of,' I said.

'Does she know?' he asked.

'No.'

'Maybe you'd feel better if you told her.'

I could just see myself telling Lisa that! I shook my head at Dr Holland.

He gave me a small laugh. 'Well, you'll be just fine, Tony. There's no real problem here.' He stood up and patted me on the back. Then he opened the door to his waiting room and called in my mother. I read a magazine while she talked to the doctor.

Everybody was nice to me at home that day — even Maxine. She made my favourite kind of chicken for supper. While we were eating it my mother told us that the stores were decorated for Christmas already. And that since this was to be our first Rosemont Christmas she wanted it to be extra special.

'Make me a list of what you want, Tony,' my mother said.

'I thought I was supposed to mail that list to Santa,' I said.

My mother laughed. 'Listen to him!' Then she said, 'Not so many years ago you did write to Santa!'

'I'll tell you one thing,' my father said. 'This is going to be the first Christmas I've ever had where I don't have to worry about the bills. This year we can afford to splurge!'

'I really don't know what I want,' I said. 'But I'll think about it.'

Later I took my pill and got ready for bed. I kneeled in front of my window until ten o'clock but Lisa's room stayed dark. When I got into bed I thought, if I had binoculars I could see her really good – up close – her face and everything. I knew what to put on my Christmas list.

That night I dreamed about Lisa. My dream went on and on. It started out at the football game where Lisa put her arm around me. Only in my dream she didn't stop there. And Corky was in it too. She was sitting on the football field and Lisa kept saying, 'You see, Corky . . . here's what to do . . . to do . . . to do . . .'

I woke up suddenly. It was morning. I felt wet and my pyjamas were sticky. Oh God! There is something wrong with me. *Really wrong*. Dr

Holland doesn't know what he's talking about! I am *so* sick. This proves it.

Wait a minute. Wait just a minute. Maybe I had a wet dream. Yeah . . . I'll bet that's it. How about that? I thought they'd be different though. I thought a lot more stuff would come out. And anyway, I wasn't sure I'd ever have one. At least not yet.

What am I supposed to do? Maybe I should stay in bed all day. But then my mother might call the doctor and he'd probably tell her the truth. I better get up. But what about my pyjamas? I guess the first thing to do is get undressed. Okay . . . I will.

I threw my pyjamas into the hamper in my bathroom. I soaked a washcloth and threw that in too. Then I mixed up all the dirty clothes so everything would feel damp, not just my pyjamas.

When I went back into my room I sat down on my bed. There was a spot on my sheet. I touched it. It was damp! Oh no – does that stuff stain? I grabbed some tissues and wiped it up.

Will Maxine know? I suppose I could change my sheet . . . but that would look worse, wouldn't it? Then she might think I wet my bed like a little kid. No . . . leave the sheet on and check it first thing after school to make sure nothing shows up.

I had an awful day. I couldn't concentrate on my school work and I got yelled at in English class for not paying attention. How could I pay attention? I kept thinking that when I get home the whole family's going to be there. Mom and Pop, Grandma, Ralph and Angie, Vicki, Maxine, even cousin Ginger! They'll all know about me. Maxine will show them the sheet and my mother will say, 'I don't buy the best sheets for you to mess up, Anthony!'

I'll say, 'It was an accident, Mom . . . a mistake . . . it won't happen again.'

And Ralph will say, 'If you hadn't been thinking about that girl this never would have happened.'

Then Pop will say, 'I expected great things from you, Tony . . . and this is what I get!'

After school I rushed home. Nobody was waiting for me. My mother wasn't even home. What a relief! I ran up to my room, closed the door behind me and pulled down my bedspread and blanket. The sheets were changed! There were striped ones on my bed this morning and now they were plain blue. Does that mean Maxine knows? Did she tell my mother? Or . . . wait a minute . . . is this the day the sheets get changed every week? I can't remember! I don't think I'll ever be able to look at Maxine again.

Chapter 6

Finally, I handed my mother my Christmas list. That night, after supper, I heard her tell my father, 'Tony wants binoculars.'

'Binoculars?' Pop asked.

'That's what it says here.' My mother waved my list at him. 'It's the only thing he's asked for.'

'What's he going to do with binoculars?' my father asked.

All this time I was sitting on the floor leaning up against a chair, reading a book about Wilt the Stilt. Did they think I couldn't hear or what? I didn't look up from my book. I pretended to be absorbed in my reading.

'Tony . . .' my mother said. 'What are you going to do with binoculars?'

I didn't answer.

My mother repeated her question. 'I said what are you going to do with binoculars?'

This time I looked at her. 'What? Oh, binoculars . . .' I had my answer carefully planned. I knew they'd ask why I wanted them, but I had to be really casual about it or they might get suspicious. 'Watch birds,' I said.

'Birds?' my mother asked.

'Yes,' I told her. 'This spring. I want to find out all I can about birds.'

My mother smiled. 'It all goes to show,' she told my father, 'if you take a boy out of the city and put him close to nature he'll become a better person.'

I wouldn't exactly say Rosemont is close to nature but I didn't argue with my mother. I knew I'd be getting my binoculars.

I had another dream about Lisa. This time I was hiding in her closet while she was getting ready for bed. When I came out she didn't scream. She was glad to see me, like she knew I was there all along. Corky was in this dream too. She was dressed up like a cheerleader and all through the best part of the dream Corky jumped around and shouted cheers.

The next night when I started upstairs to do my homework my mother said, 'Vic . . . go on up with him.'

Now why did she say that? Why does she want him to come upstairs with me? That means something. Maybe they know about me. Maybe I talk in my sleep!

My father followed me up the stairs. When we got to the top he said, 'Tony . . . I'd like to have a talk with you. Just for a minute . . . okay?'

I looked down. My mother was standing at the

91

bottom of the stairs, smiling. 'Sure, Pop,' I mumbled.

'In private, Tony,' my father said. 'In your room.'

We walked to my room and when we were both inside Pop closed the door.

He knows! I'm sure he knows about me. I always knew he could read my mind. This proves it. Wait a minute . . . maybe it's just going to be a talk about how I'm doing in school. Or what I want to be or something easy like that. I hope so. I really do. 'Did I do something wrong, Pop?' I asked.

'No, no,' Pop said. 'Nothing like that. I just thought we'd have a little talk. You know . . . kind of man to man.'

Oh-oh . . . here it comes! I was right the first time. What'll I say? Nothing. I won't say a word. I'll let him say it. I sat down on my bed. Pop pulled my desk chair over and sat close to me. He looked around for a while, rubbing his hands together, almost like he was praying.

'Uh, Tony . . .' he finally said.

'Yes, Pop?'

'Uh . . . well . . . now that you're in seventh grade there are things you should know about.' While he was talking Pop cracked each of his knuckles.

'Yes, Pop?'

'Oh . . . I don't know . . . maybe Ralph should be the one to talk to you. He's a lot closer to your

92

age.' Pop stopped talking and looked around my room. Then he coughed a little and started again. 'You see, Tony . . . there are things you should know about girls and about babies and about . . . look, Tony, do you know anything?'

He doesn't know about my dreams, I thought. This has nothing to do with what I've been thinking about. He really doesn't know. He's more scared than I am.

'Tony . . . I asked you, do you know anything?'

'Sure, Pop,' I said.

'You do? You know about babies . . . how they're made?'

'Sure, Pop. Since third grade.'

My father looked like he couldn't believe it. 'Since third grade?'

'Sure, Pop. Big Joe told me all about it.'

'You're positive you have the right information?'

'Sure, Pop.'

'Do you know other things too, Tony?'

'Sure, Pop. A lot.'

My father looked relieved. 'Well,' he said, 'the important thing to remember is that I'm here to answer all your questions.'

'Okay, Pop. I'll remember.'

He rubbed his hands again. 'I don't know, Tony . . . I feel like I should say more. Your mother thinks there's a lot for you to learn, but I don't know what to tell you. I never told Vinnie or

93

Ralph anything. I don't even know how Vinnie learned. From his friends, I guess. And Vinnie told Ralph. So I'm not too experienced when it comes to discussing the subject. But listen, Tony . . . man to man . . . you can always come to me.'

'Okay, Pop.' I got up and stretched. My father stood up and put his arm around me.

'Hey, Tony . . . how about a quick game of chess?'

'Okay, Pop . . . I guess I can do my homework later.'

When we were downstairs my mother gave Pop a look that said, *Well?* And he gave her one back that said, *Everything's taken care of*.

The next day my father handed me a book called *Basic Facts About Sex*. He said I should read it in my spare time and if I have any questions I should come to him. There's a whole section on wet dreams and another on masturbation. Maybe they do know about me after all! My stomach jumped around so bad I had to take a pill.

We got ready for our first Christmas in Rosemont. First we bought a live tree. Not a little one – a big floor-to-ceiling one. We bought it at the high school field, where the Boy Scouts hold their annual sale. I've always wanted a real Christmas tree. In Jersey City we had a little white one that sat on top of the corner table. It looked nice but it didn't have that great smell. Frankie's family had a live tree every year and sometimes I used to just sit in his living room and sniff it for an hour.

My mother bought a million tree ornaments at Bloomingdale's, including tinsel so wide we had to wrap it around the tree instead of just hanging it from branches.

My father, being an ex-electrician, lit up the outside of our house with a lot of tiny bulbs in the bushes. They twinkle on and off. He set up spotlights to show off our front door too.

Maxine was in charge of the door. She covered it with gold foil to match the twinkles. Over the foil is a huge wreath. I have to admit, the house looks good.

My mother tried to get Grandma to come downstairs to see our tree. Once a week Mom insists she leave her room so Maxine can clean it and air it out. But instead of coming downstairs for an hour, Grandma locked herself up in my bathroom.

I told my mother, 'Grandma's not looking so good.'

And my mother said, 'How can she look good when she never gets fresh air?'

So I said, 'Maybe she'd get some fresh air if you'd let her go back to doing the cooking.'

'How would that look to the neighbours?' my mother asked, 'like she's the maid or something!'

And I said, 'Who cares about the neighbours!'

'Grandma's worked hard all her life,' my mother said. 'Now it's time for her to take it easy and enjoy herself.'

'She doesn't act like she's enjoying it,' I argued.

'Of course she is! Doesn't she love that colour TV?'

'How do I know?' I said.

'Well, she watches it all day, doesn't she?' My mother bent over to pick a piece of lint off the carpet.

'That doesn't mean she likes it,' I said. 'She just hasn't got anything better to do.'

'What do you want her to do, Anthony? Play golf with Diane Hoober!'

Oh-oh. She was getting mad now. But so was I. I shouted, 'Maybe I want her to cook!'

'That's enough, Anthony!' my mother said. 'Maxine will hear you and get insulted.'

'Maxine is a lousy cook,' I mumbled. That isn't true but I felt like saying it. I was taking Dr Holland's advice – about when you feel like saying something, say it!

'Watch your mouth, Anthony!' my mother said very low, making each word sink in. 'It's growing faster than the rest of you.'

Joel asked me to go Christmas shopping with him. I told him okay, because I have a lot of allowance saved up and I want to buy something nice for everybody in our family. Now I'm sorry I said I'd go with him. Suppose he steals something?

I feel like calling him to say, 'Forget it, I can't go.' But then he'll want to know why and what will I say?

When Joel called for me I was in the bathroom. My stomach hurt. But in a little while the pain went away and we went downtown together. Once we got to the store I followed Joel around like a detective.

Every time he put his hands in his pockets I was there to make sure he hadn't taken anything. Once we were loaded down with shopping bags I really had a hard time. I paid more attention to Joel than to my shopping list. I was surprised to see that he paid for everything. Maybe Joel never really stole those batteries. Maybe it was all my imagination. It could have been a mistake! But what about the apples at lunch? He steals one every day and that's not my imagination.

I helped Joel pick out his present for Lisa. We decided on this stretch sweater that the saleslady said fits like a second skin. Joel chose the colour – green. I liked the orange one better.

The day before Christmas a piano arrived at our house. A baby grand. Six men delivered it. It was my father's gift to the whole family, but my mother had gone along with him to pick it out, so I was really the only one surprised.

When it was all set up in front of the living room windows my mother got tears in her eyes and said, 'It's absolutely gorgeous! I've always wanted a piano. Oh Vic . . . I'm so happy!' With that she threw her arms around my father's neck and kissed him. I don't like them to act that way in front of me.

'Do you like it, Tony?' my father asked, untangling himself from my mother.

'It's really neat,' I said. 'But nobody here plays the piano.'

'Not yet,' my mother said, putting an arm around my shoulder.

I knew what was coming. Piano lessons for me. Sometimes I wish we didn't have so much money. How can I tell them I don't want piano lessons? How can I tell them I can't even clap my hands in time to music. I don't even sing in the shower – I'm *that* bad!

On Christmas morning we waited for Ralph, Angie and Vicki to arrive before we opened anything. Here's what I got: Two V-neck cashmere sweaters – the kind Joel wears – one from my parents and the other from Angie and Ralph, a set of encyclopedias and *super deluxe* extra powerful binoculars! The card said:

For our son the bird watcher . . .
with all our love
Mom and Pop

We gathered upstairs in Grandma's room to watch her open her presents. She got a robe and slippers from my mother and father — a robe and slippers from Ralph and Angie — and a silver toothbrush from me. I bought it in the department they call *'For the Woman Who Has Everything.'* Grandma doesn't have everything of course, but at least this was something different. The only time she smiled was when she opened the silver toothbrush. So I was glad I gave it to her.

That night I kneeled by my window and waited. Lisa's lights were on and her shades were up as usual. I don't think she ever bothers pulling them down. Finally she came into her room. My hands were really shaking. I couldn't even hold my binoculars steady. The view was great. Just great! It was like she was standing right in front of me. I could even see the expression on her face. She was smiling. She has a terrific smile. The first thing she did was try on the green stretch sweater. She turned around and around in front of her mirror. She doesn't have to worry. She's beautiful from every angle. I wanted to tell her that. I watched until her lights went out. I love her, I think.

The next day Mrs Hoober rang our bell and I

thought, she knows! She knows I've got binoculars and that I watched Lisa last night. She's going to tell my parents and they'll take away my binoculars and tell me I've got a dirty mind. They'll move me to another bedroom so I can't see her any more. Maybe I'll even have to spend six weeks in the Juvenile Detention Centre. If I do, I hope Lisa will come on visiting day.

But I was all wrong. Mrs Hoober only wanted to give us some candies from England and wish us a Merry Christmas. When she left she called to my mother.

'Don't forget, lunch at the club in two weeks . . . Friday. See you then, Carol.'

'Carol! Who's Carol?' I asked when Mrs Hoober was gone.

My mother laughed. 'Oh, that's what Diane calls me. She says Carmella's too hard to remember.'

'Just like Millicent! Just like their maid!'

'What's the difference, Tony?'

'Your name is not Carol!' I yelled. My mother just stared at me. *Why don't you tell her if she can't remember your name then you don't want to be her friend!*

I wanted my mother to yell back at me, but she didn't. She turned to my father and spoke very slow. 'I don't know,' she said. 'You raise them with kid gloves and then they walk all over you. What's

100

the point?' She repeated 'What's the point?' over and over as she left the room.

I ran upstairs and locked myself into the bathroom. I knew I'd get sick now. And it would be my mother's fault. She'd be sorry!

In a few minutes my father knocked on the door and called, 'You all right, Tony?'

'I'm okay,' I muttered.

'I'd like to talk to you.'

'I have nothing to say.'

'Come on, Tony . . . open up the door.'

I unlocked it and said, 'It's open.' Then I turned on the water and splashed my face. When I was through my father handed me a towel.

'A name's not so important, Tony,' my father said. 'What's inside you is what counts. But not a name. It's just like Tony instead of Anthony. What's the difference if Mrs Hoober wants to call your mother Carol and she doesn't mind? It's not going to change her. You hurt her, Tony. She's very upset about you.'

'I'm sorry,' I said. I felt like I did on Veterans Day when I stood over Vinnie's grave . . . guilty!

The next week I started my piano lessons. The teacher is Miss Orenberg and she comes to the house every Thursday from four till quarter to five. She has bad breath, which I reported to my mother after the first lesson.

101

'Maybe she ate something she shouldn't have,' my mother said. 'Diane Hoober says she's an excellent teacher. Lisa took lessons from her for years.'

But Miss Orenberg smelled the same the following week. When I told my mother she said she'd see what she could do. After that my mother greeted Miss Orenberg at the door with Chlorophyll candies. 'Take one,' she'd say. 'It'll refresh you for Tony's lesson.'

After the fourth lesson Miss Orenberg asked me did I practise much. I told her about fifteen minutes a day. Miss Orenberg said she found that hard to believe. And I told her if she didn't believe me she could ask my mother because it was true. Then she said I wasn't progressing as fast as she had hoped I would. And I said that was because I wasn't musically inclined and I really didn't want piano lessons in the first place. I wanted to add that I didn't like her, or her breath or the way she talked, but I didn't.

That night I told my mother that I was never going to learn to play the piano and there was nothing she could do about it and that if she made me take any more lessons my pains were going to get worse! And why didn't she ask Dr Holland if it was good for me to have to take piano lessons when I didn't want to at all!

The next day Pop said, 'Tony . . . your mother

and I have decided that if you don't want to take piano lessons you don't have to.'

'Really?' I asked. 'You really mean it?' I looked at my mother. She didn't answer me but she nodded her head a little.

Pop said, 'We're not going to force you to do something you hate. I just wish you'd remember that we only want you to have every opportunity we couldn't give your brothers.'

I wanted to say to let me alone and stop trying to shove everything that Ralph and Vinnie didn't have down my throat! But I couldn't say it because that would have hurt their feelings and they weren't trying to be mean. But sometimes they're so full of bull they make me sick.

Chapter 7

My parents joined the Newcomers Club at church. They went to a couple of parties and said they met a lot of nice people. But they still haven't been invited to the Hoobers' house and I think my mother would rather go there than all the other places put together.

Father Pissaro the Second visits Grandma every week. I go to confession once a month, same as in Jersey City. I've thought a lot about what to confess. For a while I thought I should tell him about Lisa. But I decided that watching her at night isn't really a sin. As long as it doesn't hurt anyone what's so wrong about it?

There are a couple of things I'd like to talk over with somebody. Not with Joel though and not with Marty Endo or Scott Gold either. Whenever we have a discussion it always turns into a big joke. Maybe if we still lived in Jersey City I'd ask Ralph. But I'm not sure about that either. He acts so old lately. My father said to ask *him* if I have questions but I know he's hoping I never have any. I'm thinking about going to Ted Gibbons . . . to ask him if he ever had dreams like me and then find out what he did about them.

Ted is really proud of our Youth Group. And

especially our basketball team. We've only lost one game so far and even though he tells us he doesn't care who wins, because it's how you play the game that counts, I can tell he's pleased.

This coming Friday night we're playing the First Methodist Youth Group. They're the only other team in the league that's lost just one game. Ted said he's going to bring a date to this game – some girl he really likes a lot.

I'm getting used to Corky. She doesn't bother me the way she used to. She still spends a lot of time giggling but she's turned into a pretty good cheerleader. She doesn't look anything like Lisa but she sure can yell loud! For a while she tried to sit next to me in church every Sunday but now I make sure I'm between my mother and my father so she leaves me alone.

On Friday night my father and Ralph came to see the big game. My team got to start. I was really in good form. I scored six points in foul shots alone. At the end of the first half we were leading by two points. The Methodist guys were pretty good.

In the second half Marty Endo's team took over and we dropped two points behind. Three minutes before the end of the game Marty tripped on his shoelace and fell flat on his face. Time out was called and we all ran onto the court. Marty was out cold. His mother and father were at the game and they came flying down from the stand. His mother got really upset when she saw him stretched out on the floor and she started to cry, 'Oh my God . . . oh my God!' It's a good thing Marty didn't hear her – he'd have been furious!

When Marty came to he didn't know what had happened. But when he tried to stand up he said he felt dizzy and nauseous and he had a big bump on his head. Ted said it could be a concussion so Mr and Mrs Endo decided to take Marty straight to the hospital.

With only three minutes left to play and our team down two points Ted called me. 'Go on in, Tony. Do your stuff.'

Corky squealed when she saw me running in and started cheering like crazy. I didn't even have a chance to get nervous. Because I wasn't on the court for twenty seconds when this big guy from First Methodist gave me an elbow in the stomach. The referee blew his whistle and called a personal foul.

It was very quiet. Everybody was watching me. I thought about Ted and about Marty and how much we'd all like to win this game. Then I aimed and threw the ball, nice and easy, the way Ted said to do it when you're under pressure. Right in the basket! The crowd started yelling and some of the guys patted me on the backside. We were only one point behind.

First Methodist had the ball. They were stalling, passing it back and forth, when Gregg Kusiv jumped up and intercepted. Now it was our ball. When we got within shooting distance of our basket Gregg passed the ball to me. I dribbled around but I couldn't shoot – I was being guarded by the biggest guy on their team. I wanted to make a basket so bad! I wanted to be the big hero! But I had no chance – so I passed it to Jim Quinn and he put it in just as the whistle blew to end the game.

WE WON! WE WON! Our whole Youth Group ran onto the court and we all jumped around and hugged each other. When Ted stepped out Corky led us in a cheer just for him. Then I saw this blonde girl come rushing at Ted. She threw her arms around him and gave him a big kiss and we all stopped cheering to watch Ted and his girlfriend and that's when it hit me. The girl was Lisa! My Lisa, standing there kissing Ted . . . right in public . . . for everyone to see. Ted and his moustache! It wasn't fair. She should have been kissing me! I'm the one who won the game. Well, I did . . . didn't I? Who knows what would have happened if Marty hadn't tripped over his shoelace and knocked himself out. *Who knows?*

While I was thinking about that Corky asked me to go out for ice cream with her and some other kids from our Youth Group. But all of a sudden I didn't feel like celebrating anything. So I told her, 'Some other time maybe.'

And she said, 'Oh Tony!' and I knew she was really disappointed but I didn't care much.

I went home with my father and Ralph and even though they kept saying how great I played I didn't want to hear it.

I called up Mrs Endo to see how Marty was and she said he was very groggy but that the doctor promised he'd be okay in two days. I said I was glad to hear that. Then I told my family how tired I was from the big game and I went up to my room and fell asleep.

I tried not to think about Lisa. I didn't feel like having any dreams. I just wanted to sleep and forget about everything. But I dreamed about her and Ted and the things they probably do when they're alone and I knew I'd never ask Ted any of the questions I was thinking about asking him.

Towards the end of February Frankie Bollino called. I couldn't believe it at first.

'Hey Frankie! Is it really you?' I asked.

'None other,' Frankie said.

I asked him about my old paper route, which he reported was doing fine – about the old basketball game, which they were still playing – about junior high, which he said wasn't so bad – and about the weather, which was dumb because it was the same as in Rosemont, except we get more snow than Jersey City.

After that I didn't have anything else to say but Frankie did. 'Why don't you come back to see us some time?'

I said, 'Why don't you come see me?'

Then we both laughed until Frankie said, 'Okay. When?'

'When what?' I asked.

'When should I come see you?'

I said, 'Are you serious?'

He said, 'Sure.'

I said, 'Hey, that's great! Why don't you come on Saturday and stay overnight?'

He said, 'Swell.'

'Wait a second while I tell my parents,' I said. I put down the phone and ran into the other room.

'Guess who's on the phone?' I asked my mother and father. 'It's Frankie Bollino! I invited him to stay overnight this Saturday.'

My father said, 'I'll pick him up in New York . . . at the station. That'll save him a train ride out here.'

'Thanks, Pop,' I called, already on my way back to the phone. I picked up the receiver and said, 'Hey Frankie . . . it's all arranged. My father'll pick you up at the station in New York, Saturday.'

'What time?' Frankie asked.

'Oh . . . whatever time you say.'

'How about eight?'

'In the morning?'

'Too early?' Frankie asked.

'Yeah . . . better make it around ten.'

'Okay, Tony. See you then.'

'Right,' I said and hung up.

I really felt good. I wondered why I haven't thought about calling Frankie. I'm sure glad he called me. I went into the living room. 'How about that?' I said. 'Good old Frankie Bollino.'

'You've got plenty of friends in Rosemont,' my mother said. 'I don't see why you have to start up with him.'

'What's that supposed to mean?' I asked.

'I've got nothing against Frankie,' she said. 'It's just that Jersey City is a long way off and you can't see each other very often so you might as well concentrate on your new friends.'

But my father said, 'There's no friend like an old friend! Right, Tony?'

To be honest I have to admit that I hardly ever think about Frankie and the other guys anymore. I don't really miss them. Still, I'm looking forward to Frankie's visit.

I rode into the city with my father on Saturday morning. Frankie was already there, waiting at the station. He was carrying an airline bag. He recognized our car right away and ran straight over. 'Hey, old pal!' he hollered.

110

'Hey, Frankie!'

We sat in the back on the way home to Rosemont and when my father pulled into our driveway, Frankie let out a low whistle and said, 'Wow! You sure have come a long way!'

'Never mind the house,' I said, embarrassed. 'Come on in.'

My mother was waiting for us. 'Hello, Frank.'

Frankie dropped his airline bag on the floor and said, 'Hiya, Mrs Miglione.' He kept looking around at the house saying 'Wow!' and shaking his head.

'Well, it's nice to see you, Frank,' my mother said. I knew what she was thinking. That he didn't shake hands like certain other persons we know.

'My mother says to tell you she sends regards and when are you coming back to Jersey City for a visit,' Frankie said.

'Oh, well . . . I've been busy,' my mother said. 'You know Ralph and Angie had a baby . . . and I've been helping out.'

'This is some place!' Frankie said.

'Come on . . . cut it out, will you!' I said, giving Frankie an elbow in the ribs. 'It's just a house.'

Later I asked him how Mrs Gorsky was and he told me she says I was the best paper boy she ever had. And that she misses me a lot.

'That's crazy!' I told Frankie. 'She hated me.'

'Well, now she hates *me*,' Frankie said. 'Say . . .

111

where's your grandmother? Doesn't she live with you anymore?'

'Oh sure,' I said. 'But she stays in her room most of the time. She . . . she doesn't feel too well.' I don't think I'll ever tell anyone the truth about Grandma. I'm too ashamed.

Maxine made my favourite chicken for supper. Did she give me a special look when she served it? I'm not sure. I try to stay out of her way these days. I always bend my head when she comes into the dining room so she can't look me in the eye. I can't tell if she knows about me or not. My sheets don't get changed every time I have a dream but it seems to me Maxine smiles a lot more than she used to – and always when I'm around.

'*Wow!*' Frankie said. 'This is just great food, Mrs Miglione.'

'Thank you, Frank. We'll have to tell Maxine how much you enjoyed it. She does all the cooking.'

'You know,' Frank said for about the millionth time, 'this is really some place you have here.' He drank half a glass of milk. 'My mother said I should be sure to notice all the little things so I can tell her all about it.'

After supper Joel called and invited me and Frankie over. My father announced that he and my mother were going to a movie and that we could come along if we wanted to.

112

'What are you going to see?' I asked.

'*The Last Stranger*,' my mother said.

'What's it about?' I asked.

'Love.'

I looked at Frankie. 'No thanks,' I said. 'We'll go to Joel's.'

I think Frankie was even more impressed with Joel's house than mine. It's bigger and of course there are spotlights to show off the pool in the backyard.

Frankie couldn't believe the Hoobers' bedroom. He said, 'Wait till I tell my mother about this!'

I thought maybe I'd be able to see Lisa, but she was already out on a date. She goes out just about every Saturday night and sometimes on Fridays too. I know because I waited up for her once or twice but she's been coming in later and later. And she doesn't go out only with Ted. I can tell by the different cars that pick her up. Now I only get to see her four or five times a week.

We went into Joel's room where he showed Frankie his paperback collection. Frankie said it's even better than Big Joe's.

After that Joel asked, 'You guys want some beer?'

'What . . . are you kidding!' I said.

'No, I mean it. Didn't you ever drink beer?' Joel said.

'You know I didn't,' I told him.

Frankie said, 'Me neither. But I'll try it . . . if Tony does too.'

So we followed Joel down to the recreation room where there's a really fancy bar with barstools and everything. We started with one can. Joel had some first, then passed it to me. I choked and passed it to Frankie. We had another can when we polished off that one and then Joel asked us did we want to taste something even better.

Frankie said anything would be better than that. So Joel got out four bottles and lined them up on top of the bar. Scotch, rye, vodka and brandy. He said we'd have to drink from the bottles because if we messed up any glasses his father would know we'd been fooling around.

We started with the scotch, which burned my throat. Then the vodka, which Joel said has no taste at all and should be gulped because it would make us feel good really fast. Then the rye, which burned my throat some more. After that Joel passed around the brandy because he said that was for after dinner.

That's when Frankie fell off the barstool and started to laugh. Wow! I never heard such a crazy laugh. I mean, he just stretched out on the floor and laughed like a nut!

'Who's your friend?' Joel asked me.

'I dunno. I never saw him,' I said. It was hard to get the words out.

'Me neither. Mussbe some drunk!'

'Yeah. Mussbe.' I got off my barstool and sat down on the floor next to Frankie. 'Hey, Misser . . . you some drunk or what?'

Frankie just laughed, so I started laughing too. But when I lay down on the floor the whole room started spinning – around and around and around. I couldn't make it stop for anything.

'Hey, Joel . . . the room's going round. Commere and see.'

So Joel stretched out next to us and he said, 'Yeah . . . sure is. All aroun . . . all aroun and aroun and aroun . . . like a merry-go-roun.'

'I tole you,' I said. 'Din I tell you? Whole room's goin roun!'

'Yeah,' Joel said. 'You tole me. Know what?'

'What?' I said.

'I don feel so good.'

'Me neither.'

'Les go outside . . . get some air.'

Since Frankie was still laughing me and Joel had to lift him up and drag him over to the back door. We went outside with no coats or anything.

'Oh nice.' Joel said. 'Thas so nice.'

'Real nice,' I said. 'Good clean air.'

'Know what?' Frankie said. 'Is cold out here.'

'Yeah,' I said. 'Nice cold clean air.'

'Know what?' Joel said. 'I think I'm gonna be sick.'

'No kiddin?' I said. 'Me too.'

'Les be sick together,' Joel said.

'Sure, les be sick in the bushes,' I said.

Joel said, 'Yeah. The bushes is a good place to be sick. Is good for the bushes . . . like fertilizer.'

All three of us were sick together. When we finished I grabbed Frankie and pulled him home by the sleeve. Was it cold out!

When we got to the front of my house Frankie said, 'Wait one more minute, Tony.'

I was freezing and feeling pretty bad besides. 'What now?' I groaned.

Frankie laughed and said, 'I'm gonna fertilize your bushes too.'

Well, we made it into bed and we weren't sick again but the next morning I told Frankie he looked green and he told me that if I thought *he* looked green I should just see me. So we staggered to the mirror together and discovered we were both kind of green. Only it didn't feel as funny as it sounded. Besides my colour, my head felt like six hammers were trying to split it open at once.

Since it was Maxine's day off nobody bothered us about getting up and having breakfast. We finally managed to get dressed around noon. Then we had to sneak next door for our jackets.

Frankie left late in the afternoon after telling me and my parents what a great time he'd had. Privately he told me what a terrific town Rosemont was and he sure wished his father could strike it rich too.

At the front door my mother took a good look at us and said, 'You sure you're all right, Frank?'

Frankie said, 'Sure thing, Mrs Miglione.'

'I don't know,' she said, shaking her head. 'You both look like you're coming down with something.'

The following Saturday I had to put on my best sports jacket and tie because me and my father were going to lunch with J.W. Fullerbach. I hate ties. They choke me. I have trouble swallowing my food when I'm wearing one.

Why do I have to waste a sunny Saturday anyway? Why can't I stay home and loaf around – or play ball – or even go to a movie? Because J.W. Fullerbach wants to meet me, Pop says. Why should *he* want to meet *me*? I can't figure it out.

When I was all ready my mother inspected me. She even looked inside my ears and checked my fingernails about twenty times. I offered to take off my shoes and socks so she could look at my toenails too but she didn't think that was very funny.

'You'll remember to shake hands and say *sir*!' she reminded me.

'How could I forget that?' I asked.

We drove into the city and met Mr Fullerbach at his club. I expected him to be very big, with silver hair and powerful hands. But he turned out to be short and pudgy. My father is much taller and looks more like J.W. Fullerbach as I'd imagined him than J.W. Fullerbach really looks himself. Besides being three-quarters bald, Mr Fullerbach has a twitch in his right eye. I tried to hide my surprise at his appearance. I shook hands and said, 'I'm very happy to meet you, *sir*,' in best Rosemont style.

'So this is the youngest Miglione! Right, Vic?'

'That's him, J.W.' my father said.

'Well, Tony,' Mr Fullerbach said. 'Your father's a very smart man. But you know that, don't you?' He put an arm around my father's shoulder. 'Did you know since your father sold me the rights to his electrical cartridges we've moved up seventeen points on the market?'

I smiled.

'What do you think of that, Tony?' Mr Fullerbach asked.

'It's very good,' I said, 'sir.'

'Yes, it's good all right!' Mr Fullerbach laughed. 'Right, Vic?'

'Right, J.W.'

When we sat down to lunch I didn't know what to order because the menu was all in French. But Mr Fullerbach told the waiter to bring three steaks medium rare, so I didn't have to worry. If you ask me my father was just as relieved as I was.

Mr Fullerbach attacked his food. He washed every mouthful down with water. His glass was refilled four times just during the steak. We had vanilla ice cream for dessert. Mr Fullerbach didn't ask us if we wanted it, he just ordered. I'd have preferred chocolate chip mint, but I ate my vanilla. Mr Fullerbach reached over and patted my hand. 'Some day, Tony . . . some day I hope you'll join the company too. After college of course.'

'Of course,' I said, 'sir.'

'Yes, that will be nice. You'll join us just like your brother Ralph.' He waved his spoon at me. 'I haven't got any sons of my own you know.'

Ralph! I thought. What's he talking about? What does he mean about Ralph joining the company? That's crazy! I couldn't wait for lunch to be over. I wanted to be alone with my father. I wouldn't dare come right out and ask about Ralph in front of Mr Fullerbach. But after lunch they each smoked a whole cigar and had two brandies. I couldn't even look at the brandy. Just the smell was enough to remind me of last week and Joel's party. I excused myself and went to the men's room.

Finally Mr Fullerbach said goodbye and we thanked him for the delicious lunch and at last I was alone with my father on the expressway back to Rosemont.

'What did he mean about Ralph?' I asked.

'Ralph is going into the business.'

'How can he do that? He's a teacher! What about his job?'

'Oh, he'll finish out the school year and start over the summer.' My father never took his eyes off the road.

Why? *Why?* I wanted to scream. Ralph isn't even scientific. Everybody knows that! I wanted to grab the steering wheel and pull up the emergency brake and stop the car with a huge jerk. I wanted to yell at my father, *Go ahead and tell me the truth. Ralph's selling out.* SAY IT . . . SAY IT!

I managed to avoid Ralph for a month. I said I was too busy to go to Queens on Sundays – I had homework to do. When I heard Ralph was going to drop over I'd drop out – to the library, to Joel's, to the movies.

Then I found out Ralph and Angie were looking for a house in Rosemont – that the apartment in Queens was getting crowded – that Vicki needed a room of her own. I knew I wasn't going to be able to get away with pretending my brother didn't exist. The next time he came over I decided to stay home.

'Hi, Kid,' Ralph said, trying to box me. 'Long-time-no-see!'

'I've been busy,' I said, stepping away from him.

'Did you hear we're looking for a house?' Ralph asked, picking up Vicki and holding her up to the ceiling.

'I heard.'

'Did you hear I'm going in with Pop?' Now he shook Vicki up and down trying to make her laugh.

'I heard.' Vicki didn't laugh. She started to cry.

'Well, Kid . . . you don't sound very glad.' Ralph put Vickie back in her infant seat. 'You'll be able to see us every day if you want to . . . like the old days!'

Who cares? I wanted to yell. Who cares about seeing you every day! I felt like grabbing Ralph and shaking him. I wanted to ask him where was The Wizard. To yell, Hey Ralph . . . you stink! You're a sellout. You've gone soft – just like Mom – just like Pop – just like Angie!

Instead I said, 'Excuse me please.' And I ran upstairs to the bathroom.

I had awful pains.

On my way up the stairs I heard Ralph ask, 'What's with the Kid?'

A year ago he wouldn't have had to ask. He'd have known!

In the bathroom I considered leaving Rosemont to make my own way in the world. I could probably go to Jersey City and get my paper route back. But that was dumb! I'd never do it. It was just a thought. Anyway, I don't want to live in Jersey City again.

When I calmed down enough to unlock the bathroom door I went down the hall to Grandma's room. I haven't been in there for at least two weeks. Sometimes I forget she even lives with us. I stood there for a while, thinking that me and Grandma have a lot in common. We're both outsiders in our own home.

I knocked on the door and called, 'Grandma.' When Grandma opened it and saw me she turned off her TV. Then she sat down in her chair and held her hands out to me. I went to her. I started to cry. I kneeled down and buried my head in her lap. She stroked my hair. For a minute I felt like a little kid again. Grandma used to hold me like that when I fell down or when I was scared.

✳

Chapter 8

It didn't snow once in March. I was hoping it would. Joel got a toboggan for his birthday and he said the next time it snows we can try it out at the country club. Their golf course has plenty of hills. Now it looks like we'll have to wait until next year.

I keep remembering last March and all that rain. My mother sent my winter jacket to the cleaner early this year. She got me something new called an in-between coat to wear instead.

After school me and Joel, Marty Endo and Scott Gold started hanging out at The Bon Sweete Shop. If the weather is too bad for bikes we can walk. We always sit at the same table and always have the same waitress. She has this wild red hair and she chews gum. Her name is Bernice. She doesn't like us – you can tell. But she has to wait on us just the same. She stands there with her hands on her hips, cracking her gum and asks, 'What you kids gonna put away today?'

Usually we have milkshakes. Sometimes Marty Endo has a hamburger *and* a milkshake. He has this thing about hamburgers. I mean, he really loves them! First he smells the meat. Then when he's done smelling it he eats it, making these little noises the whole time. He calls them his happy noises.

One reason Bernice doesn't like us is we're sloppy. Somebody always spills something on the floor. The other reason is the tip. Joel thought up this idea of leaving Bernice's tip in the bottom of a milkshake glass. Every day we put it in a different glass, so she has to hunt for it. One day we didn't have any change except pennies. So we chipped in ten pennies apiece and put them in the bottom of Joel's chocolate milkshake glass which wasn't quite empty. Bernice really hollered when she saw it. By that time we were paying the cashier and getting ready to leave.

Bernice ran over to us and grabbed me by the collar. She's pretty big and I had to look way up to see her face.

'You lousy little kids! I oughta tan your hides! I oughta . . .'

'Get your hands off my friend!' Joel said. 'Or I'll call the manager.' He sounded like he meant it – no fooling around.

Bernice growled, 'You'd like that, wouldn't you! You'd like to see me get fired! What do you little rich kids know about earning a living? You think it's funny to make me fish around for a few lousy pennies? Well, let me tell you something. I *need* that money. And there's no place you can stick it that I won't reach in to get it! Your crummy forty

124

pennies buys me a loaf of bread. Did you ever think of that!'

All this time Bernice still had me by the collar and I thought I was going to strangle. But as soon as she finished her speech she let me go. We got out of The Bon Sweete Shop in a hurry.

After that we never sat at a table in Bernice's section and we left our tip on the table – not in a milkshake glass. None of us ever mentioned the incident, but I know I thought about Bernice buying that bread with our pennies for a long time.

One afternoon I needed some notebook paper so I stopped into the corner store next to The Bon Sweete Shop. Joel was with me. I decided as long as I was in the store I needed a new ballpoint pen too. My old one leaks on my fingers and smudges a lot. The pens were displayed in a mug, practically in front of the cash register. While I was deciding what colour pen to buy Joel picked two out of the mug and put them in his pocket. I think he took one ballpoint and one felt tip. They each cost 49 cents. Joel didn't look at me. He didn't look at anybody. He just smiled his crooked smile and kind of hummed a little tune.

I was furious. I mean really furious! I wanted to punch Joel in the nose. I wanted to mess up his angel face – to see the blood ooze out of his nostrils and trickle down his chin. I wanted to look him in the eye and say, 'I've had it with you, Joel! You stink! Who do you think you're fooling? You think I'm afraid to tell the manager, don't you! Well, I'm not!' Then I'd beckon with my finger and call, 'Sir . . . sir.'

'Yes, young man?' the manager would say, running towards me. By that time I'd have Joel by the back of his collar the way Bernice had me that day. 'I've caught one of those shoplifting kids, sir,' I'd say. 'If you'll check his pockets you'll find two pens. A blue ballpoint and a black felt tip.' The manager would check and pull out the pens. Then he'd call the police. The police would arrest Joel and drag him off to the Juvenile Detention Centre. My picture would make the front page of the *Rosemont Weekly*.

Soon after I would be beaten up in the boys' room and left bleeding on the cold floor. My attackers would never be caught and I would live in fear forever.

When we left the store Joel was still smiling but I was doubled over with pain. I must have caused quite a commotion. I think I fell onto the sidewalk clutching my stomach and a lot of people gathered around me.

Joel was the one who phoned my mother from the corner store. My mother rushed me to Dr Holland's office. He admitted me to the North Shore Hospital.

★

I ended up in the children's ward and was the second oldest person there. The oldest was a boy of fifteen who had his leg in traction and told me he'd be like that for two months and that he'd never ski again as long as he lived. He told me this from his bed across the room. At that time I was flat on my back being fed intravenously through a vein in my foot, which didn't hurt but wasn't exactly fun either.

Of course this wasn't the first thing that happened. What I remember first is my mother bending over my hospital bed moaning, 'Tony . . . Tony . . .' the way she says, 'Vinnie . . . Vinnie . . .' on Veterans Day. So right away I figured I was dying.

The first two days my mother stayed with me all the time. Then Dr Holland suggested she come only during regular visiting hours so the hospital routine wouldn't be upset.

I have three doctors. Dr Holland, who promised me I'm not going to die yet; a specialist named Dr Riley, who's in charge of my intestines; and a psychiatrist named Dr Fogel, who says that I'm not crazy, because when I heard he was a shrink I thought I was. And I wasn't the only one. My mother nearly had a fit.

She said, 'There's nothing wrong with Tony's mind. He's not crazy. And I don't want any psychiatrist asking him a lot of questions. They're the ones that make you crazy with their crazy questions.'

My father said, 'Carmella, Dr Fogel is going to help Tony with his problems.' He was much calmer than my mother.

'What problems? A thirteen-year-old boy doesn't have any problems! These doctors just want your money, Vic. In Jersey City this would never have happened. He's got some gas pains. That's all.'

'Mom!' Ralph said. 'You're making matters worse by discussing this in front of Tony.'

My mother looked at me. 'So now I'm crazy too!' She gave a funny laugh that sounded more like a hiccup. 'Maybe I need Dr Fogel,' she said.

'I like him,' I told her. 'And I'm not crazy!'

'Of course you're not,' my mother said. 'What a thing to say. Don't even think about it.' With that she got up off the foot of my bed and made a face at my father and brother like it was their fault I mentioned such a terrible thing.

I stayed in the hospital ten days. I slept an awful lot. Probably because they fed me so many pills. A lot of tests were done on me too. Sometimes they lasted all morning. I had to drink barium again. My insides were X-rayed. I had four separate blood tests – two from my arms and two from my fingers. I wasn't allowed to eat anything but soft, mushy foods like boiled eggs and Jello.

Mom, Pop and Ralph came to see me every day.

Angie came every other day. I received eleven pairs of pyjamas. One pair from my Aunt Rose and Uncle Lou. One pair from my twin uncles and aunts. Two pairs from Mrs Hoober. Two pairs from Angie and Ralph. Four pairs from my mother and one pair from Marty Endo and Scott Gold.

I got six books, four games and two bunches of flowers – one from my formroom class with a card everybody signed – and one from my Youth Group. I also got a pair of knitted bedroom slippers from Grandma – they itched my feet. And a photo album from Maxine. Maybe she thought I could put my X-rays in it. Joel sent me a card and included a pen in the envelope. I think it was the felt tip one he stole. Corky wrote me a letter.

Dear Tony,
I am very sorry to hear that you're sick. I hope
you'll be better soon. I really mean that. I miss
you a lot. Formroom isn't any fun when you're
absent. I really mean that, even if you don't care
about me. Because even if you don't I still
care about you. And I mean, REALLY!
Because I think you're swell. And that's the truth.

I hope when you get better you'll come to a party
I'm planning. I don't know when it will be.
Maybe not until the summer. But I'm planning it
anyway. Except I wouldn't even have it if you

129

weren't better or if you won't come. Because I
think you're the nicest boy I know and that's the
truth. So please get well soon and I really mean
that.
Love and things
Corky
(Kathryn Thomas)

I didn't tear up her letter. Maybe some day I'll feel like reading it again.

The best visitor of all came on the sixth day – Lisa. I couldn't believe it when I saw her walk in. First I thought she was there to see somebody else. But she came right over to my bed. She ruffled my hair and pulled up a chair.

She said, 'Joel couldn't come because he's too young. You have to be at least fourteen. So I'm here in his place. He sent you this . . .'

She handed me a brown bag and I took it. Inside was a paperback book full of clips and underlinings.

'He's been working on it just for you,' Lisa smiled. 'But I think you'd better hide it . . . maybe under your pillow or something . . . Here, let me . . .' she said, bending over and slipping the book under my pillow. She was so close I could smell her. She smelled really nice . . . like spring.

Right then was the perfect time for me to tell Lisa that I love her. That I've been watching her since Thanksgiving. That I'm really older than she thinks because I started school three years late since my real family are gypsies who roam the world. I was adopted by the Migliones who brought me to Rosemont. And even though we're the same age (almost) I've had so much experience – much more than her – that we'd be perfect together. When I get out of the hospital we can run off and never be seen again. We'll live on some deserted island and all we'll wear is flowers.

I must have dozed off while I was thinking these things because when I woke up it was dark and Lisa was gone.

A few days later Dr Holland told me that all my tests were fine and that my pains were functional, meaning not caused by anything physically wrong. He was turning me over to Dr Fogel who could help me get well.

When I came home from the hospital it was spring vacation so I had the week off. On Tuesday I went to Dr Fogel's office. My mother didn't come in with me. She dropped me off outside and said she'd be back in an hour.

I only saw Dr Fogel once in the hospital, but he seemed pretty nice. And I wasn't scared about my appointment because he told me when I come to his office we'll just talk.

His nurse took my name and showed me in. Dr Fogel was sitting behind his desk. 'Hello, Tony,' he said. I wondered if I was supposed to lie down on his couch. In the movies that's what people do.

So I asked, 'Where should I sit?'

He said, 'Any place you're comfortable.'

I chose the chair next to his desk and waited for him to start. He smiled at me.

'I'm glad I'm out of the hospital,' I said. 'I don't like being sick.'

'Nobody does,' Dr Fogel said.

'Yeah . . . well, I really got mad at this guy I know because he took some pens from the store and he didn't pay and I didn't know what to do. And I'll tell you something . . . it's not the first time either. I mean, maybe I should report him. When I don't know what to do I get sick sometimes.'

Dr Fogel nodded.

'And then there's my mother and father . . . well, especially my mother. She really burns me up lately. You know what she did to Grandma?'

Dr Fogel shook his head.

'Well . . . she won't let her cook anymore and that's what Grandma loved to do. She's always cooked for us. So now my mother won't let her and Grandma stays up in her room all the time and she's miserable. Only she can't tell me how miserable she is because she can't talk — because she had cancer of the larynx . . . You know what?'

Dr Fogel shook his head again.

'Sometimes I think about getting cancer. One

132

time I thought my father had it and I got really scared. But the thing is . . . my mother wasn't this bad in Jersey City. At least I don't think so. Or maybe she was and I was too dumb to know it. That's where we used to live . . . in Jersey City . . . She's really a phony. My mother is really a phony. That's what I think. I'd love to tell her I think so.'

'Why don't you?' Dr Fogel asked.

'Oh . . . then she'd start bawling . . .'

'And how would you feel about that?'

'I'd feel really bad. I don't like to see her cry.'

Dr Fogel nodded and smiled.

'And I'll tell you something else. My brother is getting just like her. Otherwise why would he go into the business? What does he know about electrical cartridges?'

I got up then and walked around the room. There was a checkerboard set up on one table and a deck of cards laid out on another. I picked up a checker. 'Who plays?' I asked.

Dr Fogel said, 'Anyone who wants to. Do you feel like a game?'

'No. I like chess.' That reminded me of Pop. I fiddled with the checker some more and said, 'My father's really something. He's a good one! He just goes along with everything. Nothing bothers him. He's on top of the world. I don't know . . . I just can't figure him out.'

Dr Fogel grunted.

'What makes me mad is why should I care so much about what they do? Any of them? Like Joel . . .' I walked over to the window and looked down. 'Why should I care if he wants to steal a lot of junk?'

'But you do?' Dr Fogel asked.

'Yeah . . . it really gets me!' I walked back to my chair and sat down. 'Sometimes I think that people can see inside me . . . that they know what I'm thinking and everything. I don't want anyone to know what I'm thinking. Like that time Joel called me chicken. I didn't want to make that phone call. I know they can trace phone calls. So why should I care if Joel calls me chicken?'

'But you do?'

'Yeah . . . I guess so. And another thing . . . sometimes I wish we still lived in Jersey City and other times I'm glad we don't. You know what? I like having plenty of money. Oh – I don't know what I want!'

I stood up then. So did Dr Fogel. He said, 'Well, Tony . . . we've had a very good first session. I'll see you again next week.'

That's it? I used up the whole hour? I talked too much. I shouldn't have told him all those things. That was stupid. Next time I won't talk at all. Let him do all the talking.

When I got outside my mother was waiting in the car. I got in and she asked, 'How did it go?'

'Dr Fogel said it went good,' I told her.

'I hope so,' she said. 'He's very expensive.'

When vacation was over I went back to school. I didn't have many pains and everyone said I was looking great, especially Corky. People always say that when they know you've been in the hospital.

✵

Chapter 9

A funny thing happened to Vicki in the spring. She got better-looking. I mean as far as babies go she isn't too bad. She looks more like those pictures you see in magazines than like a plucked chicken. She's much fatter than she used to be and she laughs a lot. Even I make funny faces at her to hear her laugh. Of course I don't go near her when she needs to be changed. Neither does my father or Ralph if he can help it. Vicki is around a lot because Angie's always out with the real estate lady looking for her house.

One sunny Saturday afternoon my mother got Vicki all wrapped up in her carriage and asked me to take her around the block for a walk.

'Me?' I said. 'You want *me* to take *her* for a walk? All by myself?'

'Why not?' my mother said. 'You're her uncle, aren't you?'

'Well, yes. I mean sure . . . but . . .' I began. 'But I don't know anything about babies.'

'What do you have to know to take her for a walk? You just push the carriage.'

'Well,' I said. 'I don't know.'

'Come on, Tony,' my mother coaxed. 'I have to

get to the store for an hour. And anyway, Maxine is here if you run into trouble.'

'Well,' I said. 'I'll try it.'

'There's nothing to it. Just push the carriage and she'll fall asleep.'

So I pushed — first back and forth in our driveway to get the feel of it. I felt pretty stupid. If I hadn't known Joel was at the dentist's office I might never have done it. I could just imagine what he would think of me pushing a baby around.

Me and Joel never talk about what happened at the corner store. I don't know if he knows I saw him take the pens or what. We act just like we did before I got sick. I asked Dr Fogel do I have to report Joel? And he said, 'That's up to you, Tony.' Dr Fogel never gives me any definite answers.

As it turned out I was mighty glad I decided to watch Vicki. Because as I was pushing her around who should back out of the Hoobers' driveway but Lisa, in her mother's car. I know she's practising up for her driver's test. I also know that the first time she backed out of the garage she did it without raising the garage door first and the car went halfway through the door. The Hoobers had to get a new garage door and Lisa wasn't allowed to go out on any dates that weekend which was good for me because it meant I got to watch her that Friday *and* Saturday night.

This time she backed out okay. When she saw

me she slowed up and waved. 'Hi, Tony. You have a real live baby in there?'

'Yeah,' I said. 'My niece, Vicki.'

Lisa stopped the car, jumped out and slammed the door shut. She ran over to me, peeked into the carriage and said, 'Oh! She's adorable. I simply adore babies! I'm mad about them. I just love them!'

I got the message.

'Can I hold her?' Lisa asked.

'Well, I don't know. She's supposed to take a nap.'

'Well, can I push the carriage?'

This was really funny. Lisa asking me all these questions like I was in charge or something. If I'd known how she felt about babies I sure would have offered to take care of Vicki before this!

So I let Lisa push Vicki but I walked right alongside her. I knew I was growing because now I come up to Lisa's neck. I figure she's as tall as she's going to get and I'm just starting to grow so I'll wind up a lot bigger than her.

'Listen, Tony . . .' Lisa said. 'If you've got something to do I don't mind watching the baby myself.'

'Oh no! I couldn't do that,' I said. 'I'm responsible for her.'

'Well, I'm a responsible person, Tony,' Lisa said, glancing sideways at me.

'No. I don't think that would be a good idea.

Something might happen if I left you alone with her.'

Lisa stopped pushing and faced me. 'Listen, Tony . . . I know you know all about the car and the garage door and all that, but I wouldn't dream of letting anything happen to the baby. It's all right! Really, I can take care of her myself.'

'No!' I said so loud I startled myself.

'Well, if that's the way you're going to be about it!'

'I'll just walk along with you,' I said. 'You can pretend it's just you and the baby if you want. After all, she is my niece!'

After that we didn't have much to say to each other. Lisa pushed and I walked behind her. I considered asking Lisa why she always gets undressed with the shades up but decided that would be stupid. My story about the gypsies would have to wait too. I didn't feel this was the right time.

We walked for an hour. Last week I told Dr Fogel about my binoculars and how I watch Lisa. I told him I've even seen her naked. I thought he'd be really surprised. But all he said was, 'How does that make you feel?' So I told him the truth. I told him that I like to watch her. That it makes me excited. Dr Fogel didn't tell me to stop doing it. And I'm glad. Because I don't know if I'd be able to. I haven't told him about my dreams yet. Sometimes I want to, but I just can't.

When we got back to my house Lisa thanked me very much for allowing her to help with Vicki and I said, 'Oh, that's okay.'

She told me she'd babysit if my sister-in-law ever needed her and she'd even do it for free because the baby is so adorable. I told her I'd keep that in mind.

After Lisa went home I bent down and whispered to Vicki, 'Thanks, pal. You got me alone with Lisa. You're not so bad after all.'

My mother told me I'd done a fine job and she was proud of me.

The end of April Lisa got her driver's licence and her own Corvette – white with red leather seats. She was so excited she offered to take me and Joel for a ride.

As soon as we got out of town Lisa started doing about eighty miles an hour. I thought she was going to get us all killed.

Joel screamed, 'Hey, Lisa . . . slow down!'

Lisa laughed and her hair blew all over her face. By that time me and Joel, who were sharing a bucket seat, were hanging onto each other and making noises somewhere between laughing and crying. I closed my eyes so I wouldn't have to see the road. Lisa drove like a maniac. I vowed never to get into her car again. Not for anything! Should I be lucky enough to get out alive this time, that is.

Finally Lisa pulled off the road and came to a

screeching halt. Me and Joel untangled ourselves and he started in on her.

'You're crazy, Lisa! I always thought so, but now I know it! Didn't you learn anything in Driver Ed?'

Lisa lit a cigarette and took a long puff.

Joel said to me, 'You see, she's got a death wish!'

'I do not!' Lisa said. 'I'm very fond of being alive.'

'Well, you'd never know it,' Joel hollered. 'You keep driving around like that and you're not going to make it to eighteen.'

'Don't be silly,' Lisa said. 'I was only trying her out. I have no intention of driving around like that all the time.' She turned to me. 'You weren't afraid, were you, Tony!'

'Well, not afraid exactly . . . but I didn't like it.'

'Come off it, Tony. You were scared out of your mind,' Joel said.

'Okay . . . I was,' I admitted. 'Sure I was scared – right out of my mind.'

Lisa laughed and kept puffing away.

'If you keep on smoking you won't have to worry about getting yourself killed in this car. You'll be dead of cancer,' Joel said.

'Will you listen to him!' Liza waved her cigarette around. 'All of a sudden he's my father! Just what I need! *Another George.*'

'My grandmother had cancer,' I told Lisa. 'Of

141

the larynx. They had to take it out. Now she can't talk.'

Lisa looked me right in the eye. 'Is that true?' she asked.

'Yes,' I said. 'You can see her any time you want to. She lives with us.'

'How awful! Perfectly awful!' Lisa stubbed out her cigarette and threw it out of the car. 'She smoked, I suppose?'

'Oh yeah . . . like a fiend!' I said. Actually Grandma never smoked at all. The doctors said it was just one of those freaky things.

But Lisa took her pack of cigarettes out of her bag and flung them out of the car. 'I'm never going to touch another weed. *Never*! Imagine losing your larynx!'

'While you're reforming,' Joel said, 'would you mind driving slower on the way home.'

She did. Only sixty miles an hour. But she drove up a one-way street the wrong way and almost got us killed anyhow.

I enjoy thinking that I'm responsible for Lisa giving up cigarettes even if there's nothing I can do about her driving.

The second week in May Lisa banged up her Corvette. What happened was she bumped into a tree. She told me and Joel she couldn't imagine how the tree got there. Lisa wasn't hurt but her car

142

needs a new fender and she has to spend the next three Saturday nights at home.

Ralph and Angie are buying a house three blocks from us. 'Five bedrooms,' Angie said. And does Maxine have any friends who'd like to work for her? Maxine said she'd ask around.

'What are you going to do with five bedrooms?' I said. 'Rent them out?'

'Fill them up with kids!' Ralph said.

'We're expecting another one already,' Angie laughed, blushing. 'Didn't you guess?'

'No,' I said. 'I didn't guess.' But I thought how could I guess when you're still fat from having Vicki?

'Which is one of the reasons I'm going in with Pop,' Ralph said. 'Kids are pretty expensive. Especially when you want to give them everything.' Ralph and Angie gave each other a secret smile.

I thought, maybe that's the trouble. Maybe kids don't always want you to give them everything. I looked at Ralph. I can do that without hating him now. I can say okay, you're just ordinary, but I can't do anything about it. I'm trying to understand his feelings about wanting his kids to have everything. Maybe I'll be like that too. Then again, maybe I won't. After all, I'm me. I'm not Ralph.

Well, at least I got through thinking about all

that without getting pains. I'm learning how to handle myself. Dr Fogel will be glad when I tell him next week.

On 25 May me and Joel rode down to the Village Sports Store. Now that it's spring I need a new basketball net. Joel needs tennis balls for camp. He doesn't want to go back this summer, but he has no choice. 'I've been going to camp since I'm six,' he told me. 'I hate it.'

'So why not switch? Go to another camp?'

'They're all the same,' he said. 'At least here I know the guys already. I know what to expect.'

Lisa isn't going to be around for the summer either. She's going on a tour of the northwestern states and Canada. She'll be gone nine weeks. What am I going to do without her? I'll never be able to get to sleep!

When we got to the Village Sports Store we rested our bikes against the side of the building. Inside we browsed around. I saw a really neat fielder's mitt. It looked pretty expensive though.

Joel fiddled around with the tennis rackets. He tried out two of them pretending to have a volley with me. The reason we had to wait so long was the salesman couldn't get away from two Rose-mont ladies.

One of them said, 'But Ginny, you know how I

putt. Always to the right of the hole. So I need a putter that will send them left.'

The salesman said, 'It's your aim, ma'am. You've got to aim more to the left of the cup.'

Then Ginny said, 'It has nothing to do with her aim. It's the way she's built.'

'I don't think so,' the salesman said. 'Build has nothing to do with it. It's all aim.'

Then the lady holding the putter said, 'Suppose I take it and just try it out. Then if I still putt to the right I'll bring it back this afternoon. You can charge it to my husband's account.'

The salesman tried a smile but you could tell he was pretty burned up.

When he finally got rid of them he asked could he help us. Joel told him he was interested in a tennis racket but that he'd have to come back with his father for that. 'In the meantime I'll take two cans of good tennis balls,' Joel said.

The salesman showed him the two brands they carried and Joel picked what he wanted. He paid for them, counted his change and took the white bag with *Village Sports Store* written across it.

'Anything for you?' the salesman asked me.

'Yes,' I said. 'I need a new basketball net . . . and I'd like to know how much that neat fielder's mitt costs too.'

'Which one?' he asked. 'They're all neat . . . you'll have to point it out to me.'

145

'Okay,' I said, following him to the other end of the store where the mitts were displayed.

The salesman told me the mitt I liked was $37.50. I thought that was a lot of money for one fielder's mitt so I said I'd have to think about it. He told me to take my time thinking while he went to the stockroom for my basketball net. I walked back to the cash register where Joel was waiting. I wanted to know if he thought $37.50 was too much for a mitt. But I never asked him because he was smiling his crooked smile and humming some tune.

I thought, oh no! Please, Joel. I don't want to be sick again. I don't want to go back to the hospital. I know what you've done. I can tell by just looking at you. What'd you take this time, Joel? *What?*

This was no good. I had to calm down. I could feel my stomach tighten. I'd do what Dr Fogel taught me. I'd have a talk with myself inside my head. I know I'm tense. But I will be all right. I will *not* be sick.

'Let's go,' Joel said.

I could report him now. I could yell for the salesman and say, 'This guy stole something from your store.' I thought about doing that as I followed Joel outside. He got on his bike. Just as he was about to pedal off two men came running out of the store. One wore eyeglasses and a turtleneck. The other had red hair and freckles. They ran right up to Joel and the one with the glasses said, 'Okay, son . . . let's have the golf balls.'

They know, I thought. This is it. *This is really it.* He's swiped something and they know about it. Good going, Joel! *You idiot.*

'What golf balls?' Joel asked, looking innocent.

'Come on, son . . . I saw you take them,' red hair said.

'Saw me take what?' Joel asked.

I just stood there watching.

'Don't make this more difficult than it already is,' eyeglasses said. 'We've just installed closed circuit TV because of shoplifters. So we know you've got the golf balls.'

'I bought tennis balls,' Joel insisted. 'I bought two cans of tennis balls *and* I paid for them.'

Red hair grabbed the bag out of Joel's hand and opened it. He took out three packs of golf balls and held them up. 'Go ahead,' he called to the salesman who had waited on us. 'Make the call.'

'Oh, *those* golf balls,' Joel said, trying to laugh. But the laugh came out like a puppy's yelp. 'My father asked me to buy those for him. Here,' he said, fumbling around in his pocket and coming up with a ten dollar bill. 'I'll pay for them now. I just forgot, that's all.'

'Never mind,' red hair said. 'You should have thought about it before. It's too late now.'

'Tell them, Tony!' Joel shouted. 'Tell them I just forgot to pay!'

I didn't say anything.

'Tell them!' he screamed. 'You tell them or I'll never speak to you again!'

So don't, I thought. Who did he think he was, threatening me! I can get along without you, Joel. I just realized, I can get along fine without you!

'I hate you,' Joel whispered, looking at me. Then he turned away and began to cry. He bent over his handlebars and buried his head in his arms.

I couldn't stand another minute of it. I turned and started to walk my bike away. But the salesman called, 'Hey . . . you forgot your net.'

'My net?'

'Yes, your basketball net.'

'Oh.'

'You want it anyway?' he asked.

'Sure,' I said. 'How much is it?'

'$2.62 including tax.'

I handed him the exact amount and he gave me my package. I put it in my basket and hopped on my bike.

Red hair and eyeglasses were walking Joel back into the store.

'Did you set him up, kid?' the salesman asked.

'I didn't have anything to do with it, sir,' I told him.

'Maybe not. I have no proof,' he said. 'But if I

148

were you I'd be a lot more careful about who I run around with in the future.'

So when things finally caught up with Angel Face I had to be accused of setting him up. That's really something! Me – a criminal. Me – with my nervous stomach!

All these months of wondering what to do about Joel were over. Just like that! And not even because of me – because of a crummy closed circuit TV. I should feel relieved. I should feel happy, I told myself. But all the way home I thought . . . Good old Joel . . . that lousy creep . . . fixed up a paperback just for me when I was in the hospital . . . yeah, but if it hadn't been for him I might never have gotten sick in the first place . . . he told Bernice to take her hands off me, didn't he . . . sure he did . . . what could she do to him . . . he's my best Rosemont friend . . . at least he was . . . well, wasn't he . . . what is a friend, anyway?

By the time I got home I figured Joel would be locked up in jail. His father would get him a good lawyer though. I wondered what my mother would think about Joel being sent to the Juvenile Detention Centre. I probably wouldn't see him for years. Well, that's okay with me. I don't want to see him. The way he screamed at me. The way he cried!

That night after dinner my father helped me put

149

up my new basketball net. As I watched him work I thought, he's a lot older than most of my friends' fathers. After all, if Vinnie was still alive he'd be twenty-eight. Pop's already a grandfather. I don't know why I never thought about that before.

He still doesn't know about Joel. Neither does my mother. I decided to let them read it in the morning paper. Let them be really shocked. I can just see the headline:

ROSEMONT BOY CAUGHT SHOPLIFTING
GETS TEN YEARS

When the net was fastened my father went into the house. I stayed out and shot a few baskets. I practised dribbling and foul shots too. Then I fell onto the grass and did pushups.

'Hi, Tony.'

I looked up. I couldn't believe it – Joel! I jumped to my feet. 'What are you doing home? I thought . . . I thought . . .'

'Yeah. Well, the owner of the store isn't pressing charges.'

'He's not?'

'Nope. He called the cops and my father. I got a long lecture.'

'That's all?'

'Yeah. Since it's my first offence nobody wants me to have a record.'

'Oh.'

'That's the way it's done in Rosemont.'

'Oh.'

'I'll be back in school tomorrow.'

'You will?'

'Yeah. But next year I've got to go away to school . . . to some military academy.' Joel reached down for a blade of grass which he chewed on for a while. 'Can you see me in military school?'

I laughed but no sound came out. So I shook my head.

'Well, me neither,' Joel said. 'But that's how George Hoober deals with his problems. He puts them away some place. And right now I'm problem number one. You know . . . anything so his golf game isn't messed up!' He picked up a stone and threw it in the direction of his house. 'I only did it for fun,' he said. 'To prove I could get away with anything.'

I just looked at him.

'I told them it wasn't a setup . . . that you didn't have anything to do with it.'

Was he waiting for me to say thank you? I wasn't about to.

'Look, Tony . . . my father sent me over here to ask you not to say anything about what happened. He doesn't want it to get around.'

'I won't say anything. Why should I say anything now?'

151

'Well, thanks pal.' Joel pretended to tip his hat at me but he wasn't wearing one. 'See you around,' he called as he headed for home.

'Sure,' I muttered. 'See you around.'

The next day Mrs Hoober told my mother that Joel was going to military school in the fall because the young people of today need strong discipline and that this particular military academy was just about the best there was anywhere. And that of course Joel would get a much finer education than at Rosemont Junior or Senior High. My mother thought maybe I should go too.

'I want you to have the best possible education, Tony,' she said.

But my father looked at me and said, 'Let's leave the decision to Tony this time.'

I think he knows I'll be okay now – that I can face things.

'I want to stay at Rosemont Junior,' I told them.

I almost laughed. I almost laughed and said to my mother, 'If Mrs Hoober told you Joel was going to the Juvenile Detention Centre would you ask me if I wanted to go too?' But I didn't say it. And I didn't get any pains either. Because it was funny. Funny and sad both.

Chapter 10

Now it's 10 June. I'm riding around on my bike. I'm thinking about my birthday. That I'm going to be fourteen.

Fourteen years is a long time to have been around.

It's kind of old if you really think about it.

This afternoon they're going to break ground for our swimming pool. For the last three weeks my father's been spending all his spare time with the man from the Athena Pool Company. They've been drawing up plans – where to place the diving board – where to put the cabanas – what shape should the pool be – heated or not heated?

Our swimming pool.

The swimming pool of the Miglione family.

I pedal faster and faster till I'm almost out of breath.

You remember the Miglione family, don't you? They used to live in a two-family house in Jersey City. They used to wait on line for the bathroom.

I shift into low to get to the top of the hill. Suppose I wake up tomorrow morning and the money's all gone. Would I care? Would I?

I'm at the top of the hill now. I laugh out loud. I wonder if anybody hears me.

153

I put my feet up over the handlebars and coast all the way down. Faster and faster – scared I'll crash into the tree at the bottom, but not using my brakes.

I make it. I'm at the bottom of the hill now.

I had a funny dream last night. It wasn't about Lisa. It was about Corky only she looked like Lisa. But still, I knew it was Corky. And I wasn't just looking at her either. It was a pretty good dream. I wonder what Corky will really look like when she's sixteen? I think I'll ask Dr Fogel about my dreams. Can too many of them hurt me?

I shift gears and pedal backwards.

I think what I'll do is – I'll go home and put my binoculars away on the top shelf of my closet – over in the corner – so they're hard to get.

Then again, maybe I won't.

JUDY BLUME

JUST AS LONG AS WE'RE TOGETHER

How can you be best friends with someone who keeps secrets from you?

Rachel and Stephanie have been best friends forever . . . then Alison arrives. Alison is cool, fun and her mum's a famous actress – how can Rachel compete with that? And Rachel knows Stephanie is hiding something from her. Something big. But the truth is, Stephanie's secret is too upsetting to talk about. What she really needs are two best friends to help her deal with it.

Turn the page to read an extract

one

'Stephanie is into hunks,' my mother said to my aunt on Sunday afternoon. They were in the kitchen making potato salad and I was stretched out on the grass in our yard, reading. But the kitchen window was wide open so I could hear every word my mother and aunt were saying. I wasn't paying much attention though, until I heard my name.

At first I wasn't sure what my mother meant by *Stephanie is into hunks*, but I got the message when she added, 'She's taped a poster of Richard Gere on the ceiling above her bed. She says she likes to look up at him while she's trying to fall asleep at night.'

'Oh-oh,' Aunt Denise said. 'You'd better have a talk with her.'

'She already knows about the birds and the bees,' Mom said.

'Yes, but what does she know about boys?' Aunt Denise asked.

It so happens I know plenty about boys. As for hunks, I've never known one personally. Most boys my age – and I'm starting seventh grade in two weeks – are babies. As for my Richard Gere poster, I didn't even know he was famous when I bought it. I got it in a sale. The picture must have been taken a long time ago because he looks young, around seventeen. He was really cute back then. I love the expression on his face, kind of a half-smile, as if he's sharing a secret with me.

Actually, I don't call him Richard Gere. I call him Benjamin but my mother doesn't know that. To her he's some famous actor. To me, he's Benjamin Moore, he's seventeen and he's my first boyfriend. I love that name – Benjamin Moore. I got it off a paint can. We moved over

3

the summer and for weeks our new house reeked of paint. While my room was being done I slept in my brother's room. His name is Bruce and he's ten. I didn't get a good night's sleep all that week because Bruce has nightmares.

Anyway, as soon as the painters were out of my room I moved back in and taped up my posters. I have nineteen of them, not counting Benjamin Moore. And he's the only one on the ceiling. It took me all day to arrange my posters in just the right way and that night, as soon as my mother got home from work, I called her up to see them.

'Oh, Stephanie!' she said. 'You should have used tacks, not tape. Tape pulls the paint off the walls.'

'No, it doesn't,' I said.

'Yes, it does.'

'Look . . . I'll prove it to you,' I said, taking down a poster of a lion with her cubs. But my mother was right. The tape did pull chips of paint off the wall. 'I guess I'd better not move my posters around,' I said.

'I guess not,' Mom said. 'We'll have to ask the painters to touch up that wall.'

I felt kind of bad then and I guess Mom could tell because she said, 'Your posters do look nice though. You've arranged them very artistically. Especially the one over your bed.'

two

'I can't believe this room!' my best friend, Rachel Robinson, said. She came over the second she got home from music camp. We shrieked when we saw each other. Dad says he doesn't understand why girls have to shriek like that. There's no way I can explain it to him.

Rachel must have grown another two inches over the summer because when Mom hugged her, Rachel was taller. She'll probably be the tallest girl in seventh grade.

'I've never seen so many posters!' Rachel stood in the middle of my room, shaking her head. When she noticed Benjamin Moore she asked, 'How come that one's on your ceiling?'

'Lie down,' I said.

'Not now.'

'Yes, now . . .' I pushed her towards the bed. 'It's the only way you can really see him.'

Rachel shoved an armload of stuffed animals out of the way and lay down.

I flopped beside her. 'Isn't he cute?'

'Yeah . . . he is.'

'My mother calls him a hunk.'

Rachel laughed.

'You know what I call him?'

'What?'

'Benjamin Moore.'

'Benjamin Moore . . .' Rachel said, propping herself up on one elbow. 'Isn't that a brand of paint?'

'Yes, but I love the name.'

Rachel tossed a stuffed monkey at me. 'You are so bizarre, Steph!'

I knew she meant that as a compliment.

'Is that the bee-sting necklace?' Rachel asked, reaching

over to touch the locket around my neck. As she did her hair, which is curly and reddish-brown, brushed against my arm. 'Can I see how it works?'

'Sure.'

I stepped on a bee in July while I was at Girl Scout camp and had an allergic reaction to its sting. The camp nurse had to revive me because I went into shock. The doctor said from now on I've got to carry pills with me in case I get stung again. They're small and blue. I hope I never have to take them. I'm not the greatest at swallowing pills. When I got back from camp, Gran Lola, my grandmother, gave me this necklace. I'd written all about it to Rachel.

I opened the small gold heart. 'See . . .' I said, showing it to her, 'instead of a place for a picture inside there's room for three pills.'

Rachel touched them. 'What did it feel like to be in shock?'

'I don't remember. I think I felt dizzy . . . then everything went black.'

'Promise you'll always wear the necklace,' Rachel said, 'just in case.'

'I promise.'

'Good.' She closed the heart. 'Now . . . what about those cartons?' she asked, pointing across the room. 'When are you going to unpack them?'

'Soon.'

'I'll help you do it now.'

'That's okay,' I told her.

'You've got to get organized before school starts, Steph.' She crossed the room and knelt in front of the biggest carton. 'Books!' she said. 'You want to arrange them by subject or author?'

'This isn't a library,' I said, 'it's a bedroom.'

'I know . . . but as long as we're doing it we might as well do it right.'

6

'I don't need to have my books arranged in any special order,' I said.

'But how will you find them?'

'I recognize them by their colour.'

Rachel laughed. 'You're hopeless!'

Later, I walked Rachel home. It's funny, because when I first heard we were going to move I cried my eyes out. Then, when my parents told me we were moving to Palfrey's Pond, I couldn't believe how lucky I was, since that's where Rachel lives. Now, besides being best friends we'll also be neighbours. And moving just a few blocks away really isn't like moving at all. I think the only reason we moved is that our house needed a new roof and Mom and Dad just about passed out when they learned what it would cost.

The houses at Palfrey's Pond are scattered all around, not lined up in a row like on a normal street. They're supposed to look old, like the houses in a colonial village. Rachel's is on the other side of the pond. When we got there she said, 'Now I'll walk *you* home.'

I looked at her and we both laughed.

When we got back to my house I said, 'Now I'll walk *you*.'

Then Rachel walked me home.

Then I walked her.

Then she walked me.

We managed to walk each other home nine times before Mom called me inside.

three

The day before school started was hot and still. I was hanging out by the pond, dipping my feet into the water. That's when I first saw the girl. She was crouching by the tree with a big hole in it. I figured she was trying to get a look at the raccoon family that lives inside. I've never seen them myself, but my brother has.

I shook the water off my feet, put on my sandals, and walked over to her. She looked about Bruce's age. Her red and white striped T-shirt came down to her knees. Probably it belonged to her father. Her hair was long. She hadn't brushed it that day. I could tell by her crooked parting and the tangles at the ends. I guess she wasn't worried about stepping on a bee because she was barefoot.

She had a small dog with her, the kind that has fur hanging over its eyes. As soon as I came close the dog started to bark.

'Be quiet, Maizie,' the girl said. Then she turned to me. 'Hi . . . I'm Alison. We just moved in. You probably didn't notice because we didn't have a moving van. We're renting Number 25.'

'I'm Stephanie,' I said. 'I live here, too. Number 9.'

Alison stood up and brushed off her hands. She reached under her T-shirt, into the pocket of her shorts, and pulled out a card. I was really surprised because I'd had one just like it last week. On the front it said, *Looking forward . . .* And inside it said, *to meeting you next Thursday.* It was signed *Natalie Remo, seventh grade homeroom teacher, Room 203.*

'What do you know about Mrs Remo?' Alison asked. 'Because that's who I've got for home-room.'

I guess she could tell I was surprised. She said, 'You probably thought I was younger. Everyone does since I'm so small. But I'm going to be thirteen in April.'

I didn't tell her I'd thought she was Bruce's age. Instead I said, 'I'll be thirteen in February.' I didn't mention the date either – February 2 – Ground Hog Day. 'I'm in Mrs Remo's home-room too. She sent me the same card.'

'Oh,' Alison said. 'I thought she sent it to me because I'm new. I'm from Los Angeles.'

'My father's there now, on business,' I told her. He's been there since the beginning of August, ever since we moved. I don't know how long he's going to be away this time. Once he had to go to Japan for six weeks.

Maizie, the dog, barked. Alison kneeled next to her. 'What'd you say, Maizie?' she asked, pressing her ear right up to Maizie's mouth.

Maizie made a couple of sounds and Alison nodded, then giggled. 'Oh, come on, Maizie,' she said, as if she were talking to her dog. Then Alison looked up at me. 'Maizie is such a character! She told me to tell you she's glad we're in the same homeroom because she was worried about me not knowing anyone in my new school.'

'Your dog told you that?'

'Yes,' Alison said. 'But look . . . I'd really appreciate it if you didn't say anything about it. Once people find out your dog can talk, forget it. In L.A. there were always reporters and photographers following us around. We're trying to avoid the same kind of publicity here.'

'You mean,' I said, 'that your dog actually talks . . . like Mr Ed, that talking horse who used to be on TV?'

'That horse didn't really talk,' Alison said, as if I didn't know.

'Well,' I said, scratching the mosquito bite on my leg, 'exactly how does Maizie talk? I mean, does she talk in human words or what?'

'Of course she talks in words,' Alison said. 'But she doesn't speak perfect English because English isn't her first language. It's hard for a dog to learn other languages.'

'What's her first language?' I asked.

'French.'

'Oh,' I said, 'French.' Now this was getting really good. 'I'm taking Introduction to French this year.'

'I'm taking Introduction to Spanish,' Alison said. 'I already speak French. I lived outside Paris until I was six.'

'I thought you were Chinese or something,' I said.

'I'm Vietnamese,' Alison said. 'I'm adopted. My mother's American but she was married to Pierre Monceau when they adopted me. He's French. Mom came to the States after they got divorced. That's when she met Leon. He's my stepfather.'

I absolutely love to hear the details of other people's lives! So I sat down beside Alison, hoping she would tell me more. Bruce says I'm nosey. But that's not true. I've discovered, though, that you can't ask too many questions when you first meet people or they'll get the wrong idea. They may not understand that you're just very curious and accuse you of butting into their private business instead.

Alison fiddled with a twig, running it across Maizie's back. I didn't ask her any of the questions that were already forming in my mind. Instead I said, 'Would your dog talk to me?'

'Maybe . . . if she's in the mood.'

I cleared my throat. 'Hi, Maizie,' I said, as if I were talking to a little kid. 'I'm your new neighbour, Stephanie Hirsch.'

Maizie cocked her head at me as if she were actually listening. Her tiny bottom teeth stuck out, the opposite of mine. My top teeth stuck out before I got my braces. The orthodontist says I have an overbite. That would mean Maizie has an underbite.

'What kind of dog are you?' I asked, patting her back.

Her fur felt sticky, as if she'd been rolling in syrup.

'She's a mixture,' Alison said. 'We don't know anything about her parents so we don't know if they could talk or not. Probably not. Only one in seventeen million dogs can talk.'

'One in seventeen million?'

'Yes. That's what the vet told us. It's extremely rare. Maizie is probably the only talking dog in all of Connecticut.'

'Well,' I said. 'I can't wait for Rachel to meet Maizie.'

'Who's Rachel?' Alison asked.

'She's my best friend.'

'Oh, you have a friend.'

'She lives here, too. Number 16. She's really smart. She's never had less than an A in school.' I stood up. 'I have to go home now. But I'll see you tomorrow. The junior high bus stops in front of the lodge. That's the building down by the road. It's supposed to come at ten to eight.'

'I know,' Alison said. 'I got a notice in the mail.' She stood up too. 'Do you wear jeans or skirts to school here?'

'Either,' I said.

'What about shoes?'

I looked at Alison's bare feet. 'Yes,' I said, 'you have to wear them.'

'I mean what *kind* of shoes . . . running shoes or sandals or what?'

'Most of the kids here wear topsiders.'

'Topsiders are so preppy,' Alison said.

'You don't *have* to wear them,' I told her. 'You can wear whatever you want.'

'Good,' Alison said. 'I will.'